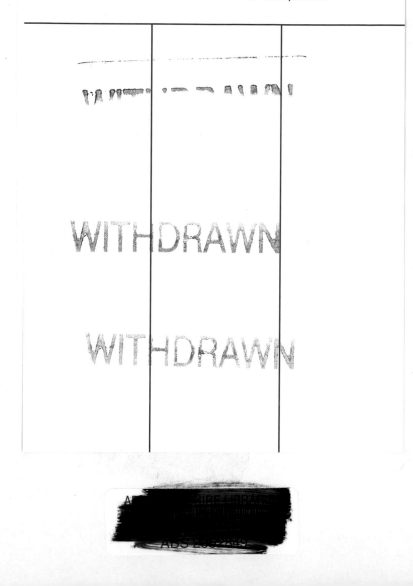

**Other Books from Scottish Cultural Press
by Kenneth C Steven**

Dan
1 898218 07 2

The Missing Days
1 898218 37 4

THE
SUMMER
IS ENDED

Kenneth C Steven

SCOTTISH CULTURAL PRESS
EDINBURGH

Published in 1997 by Scottish Cultural Press
Unit 14, Leith Walk Business Centre,
130 Leith Walk, Edinburgh EH6 5DT
Tel: 0131 555 5950 ~ Fax: 0131 555 5018
e-mail: scp@sol.co.uk

British Library Cataloguing in Publication Data
A catalogue record for this book is available from the British Library

ISBN: 1 898218 72 2

The publisher acknowledges subsidy from the Scottish Arts Council
towards the publication of this book

THE SCOTTISH ARTS COUNCIL

Printed and bound by
Cromwell Press, Melksham, Wiltshire

Kenneth C Steven was born in Glasgow but moved with his family to Highland Perthshire during his school days. He began writing early, finding the people and landscape of Scotland the primary inspiration for both poetry and prose. His acclaimed first novel *Dan* was published by Scottish Cultural Press in 1994. His first major poetry collection *The Missing Days* was published by Scottish Cultural Press in 1995 as part of its Scottish Contemporary Poets Series. Kenneth Steven is also a talented children's writer. He lives in Dunkeld.

This book is for Richard Campbell,
and also to the memory of Richard Leaf
who died long before his time.

1

Cam was still far away in his dreams when his father came to waken him. It was something to do with Rosie; he seemed to be chasing her through a thick wood and he could hear her laughing the whole time...

'Cam! Cam!'

In the end he turned round and looked up mistily at his father who was smiling faintly, the grey edges of his beard almost tickling his face. The boy frowned in the bad light of the room. It could hardly be more than six...

'Cam! I've found something! I want you to come down and have a look at it.'

Cam swam through deep seas, struggling to keep his eyes open. He loathed and detested the early morning; it was the very worst thing about living on a farm. Rain danced against the window panes.

'Will it not wait? 'S only dawn, dad!'

'Och, come on.' His father's eyes twinkled in amusement at his son, lazy as ever. 'It's worth getting up for, I'm telling you, boy! Good practice for university as well!' he added with a wink. 'I'll see you down at the bottom field, Cam. Put your boots on.'

The door closed. Cam sighed and dunted his head back into the pillows. He'd better go. He would die of curiosity if he didn't, and he was more or less awake now anyway. He flung back the bedclothes and got up, feeling the nip that was in the air now. The summer was over all right; not long now till the frost would be here. He stumbled blearily towards his clothes, shivering, and began to get dressed.

Cam passed his brother Robert's room and was on the point of going in to waken him. His hand was on the doorknob and his heart thudded with a wicked joy, but at the last moment he turned away. Robert was older and stronger; Cam had lost every fight there had ever been, and he'd be sure to get a good kick if he went in and woke him for nothing.

Robert had said hardly a thing about the place at university, in fact nothing at all. Cam thought about it now, mulling that over in his head. Rob had never even wanted to go to university himself; it would have taken ropes and horses to drag him to a city, let alone make him study there. Ardnish was all that had ever been in his head – the hills, the fields, the house, the land. Not that he would ever have said so, but he was fiercely proud of it. Maybe he was thinking of Annie again, whether he had a chance or not... Maybe that was why he was so sullen and dark these days, Cam thought.

He clattered down the stairs, deliberately making a lot of noise. After all, if he was up, why should the rest of them get two hours' extra sleep? Misty was in the hall; she stretched and wheezed when Cam came towards her. His dad must have taken Fruin instead. Misty was getting old and lazy.

'Aye, you like your chin being tickled,' Cam whispered, and bent down for his boots. All of a sudden, a picture of Fleet came into his mind and a shadow of pain went through him. He'd loved that dog like nothing else on earth. He could see her yet, the big yellow eyes like marbles, so wise and gentle; she was the only dog that had ever been his own. When Corrie had had her puppies he had been allowed to choose one for his birthday. He remembered it so clearly – hadn't it been his fourth? Fleet had lain at the bottom of his bed for ten whole years, big soft lump that she was. Cam bent to untie the laces of his boots – he must have kicked them off without bothering the night before. He yawned, and his stomach made hollow noises; he would make sure of a good breakfast when he was back from the field. Misty looked questioningly at him as he got up, and his hand passed over the tip of her nose.

'No, you stay here,' he said gently. 'Lie down! I'll be back.'

He opened the door and went out. He dug his hands into his jacket pockets and stopped in his tracks, looking out to the west at the whole world, the breath suddenly knocked right out of him. Far off he could hear the sound of the curlews, maybe a dozen or more of them; it was like the strangest singing, as though they were women, mourning lovers who had gone off to war and would never come back. He'd listened to them often enough; he'd heard that song through the bedroom window as he lay trying to sleep, but just at this moment it seemed different; it meant more than at other times. In a week he wouldn't be here any more; he'd be away in Aberdeen in a new life, surrounded by streets and night

2

life and folk from every part of the world. It was what he had wanted, wasn't it? It was what he had worked for. Yet just at this moment he wondered.

He suddenly felt as if he would be going into exile. But that was stupid; he could be back here as often as he liked. All the same, a sort of panic came over him, a feeling that nothing would ever be the same again, that things would happen here while he was away, and he would be outside of it all. He imagined his father dying, the farm being sold, a huge hotel being built down by the shore, looking out towards Shuan. Och, he was being stupid, paranoid; likely as not there'd be no great changes at all. But for a second he found himself envying Robert, with his complete contentment here, his ability to shrug his shoulders at anything but Ardnish and the life he'd always known.

I'm too restless, Cam thought to himself, I've always been my own worst enemy. He sighed, shivered slightly as a cold edge of wind came from the shore; he told himself firmly that he had a whole week left before going away and he would go round and look at things, and remember – not because he was really afraid of losing them, but simply to try to see this place as it was, instead of just blindly going round fiddling away the days...

'Are you coming before Christmas?'

Cam turned and looked down the field to the solid figure of his father. He smiled and started down more quickly towards him. The mist was lifting off the sea, moving away in white curls that were like the wisps of hair on an old woman's head. He passed the edge of the barley field and on into the next one which was under grass for hay. His father had been working away on a great mound of earth that was plumb in the middle of that field – a wart of a thing it was, with great slabs of rock sticking out at odd angles, and a strange lump of grassy ground at the top. Duncan Mackay had always told his sons it was just a heap of rocks the first farmers had dumped there to be rid of them; now he was tired of forever going round it with the machines. It was like an itchy spot on his skin and he wanted it away. A lot of the big stones had gone already; Cam had seen him staggering under the weight of slabs that must have weighed more than a hundredweight before heaving them on to the shore.

Now Cam felt an edge of excitement inside him. When he was very young he would look out of his window at that place, his eyes hovering over it; somehow it always fascinated him, almost as if he knew without being told that more was buried there than just huge slabs of stone. To him it was an ancient secret place; he could remember hiding there from Robert, crouching down like a hedgehog when they were playing hide and seek, or when Robert was on the warpath for some reason or other. It was almost as though in a funny way it was the centre of everything at Ardnish – not the house at all. But he'd never said any of that to anyone; these were just odd thoughts that filled his head now and again like thistledown, and then blew away.

His father was bending over the grassy mound, except that now the roof of it was gone, as the top might have been sliced off an egg.

'See what I've found you, Cam Mackay,' he said with a kind of boyish pride. 'This was worth getting up for, I'm telling you!'

He gestured with his head towards the mound and Cam bent down, and then involuntarily drew in his breath as he reached out to touch the thing. Clearly delineated in the earth under the top of the mound was a harp. It was still buried so that only the rim could yet be seen, as well as the strings that stretched across it. But on the surface of the wood there were the most wonderful knots and curls, with a complicated interwoven pattern which the eye followed with difficulty. The ground there was peaty, black as pitch, so rich that its scent filled the air all around. Cam gingerly touched the harp with one finger, almost as though it might crumble at his touch like that bunch of flowers they'd found in the Egyptian pyramid. But the wood was strong and smooth, as if it had been fashioned the day before. Cam just looked up at his father and stared, not knowing what to say; for a moment he even wondered whether the harp had been planted there as a kind of joke. Duncan Mackay just laughed, a delighted chuckle that expressed his pleasure at finding this treasure, and on his own land too.

'No one's taking that away to Edinburgh anyway,' he said firmly at last. 'So you'd better keep it under your hat when you're in the village. It's old all right, no doubt of that. And it'll still play! Run your hand over it, Cam – harder than that. Look! The thing's held its tune for maybe a thousand years; imagine that! Now that's better than the things they churn out in Japan, eh?'

Cam was hardly taking the words in as he crouched there; to tell the truth, he was still half-asleep and almost believed he was dreaming all this and would waken up in bed. But the wind on his face was real enough, and the wood of the harp was solid and didn't melt away when he touched it.

'You could get Martha to try playing it,' he heard himself saying, as he dared at last to pluck the strings, and the sounds were at once blown away by the wind. His father's eyes lit up like lochs in sunlight.

'That's an idea all right! Of course, Martha's got a clarsach. I'll give her a call.' He turned to go.

'Dad, have a heart – it's only six,' Cam said weakly, with a hint of reproach.

His father nodded and bent to stroke Fruin; the dog was lying on the other side of the mound, looking for all the world like a bored pupil waiting to be allowed out of school.

'On you go and get some breakfast,' Duncan said more quietly. 'I'll be in in an hour or so. I've another stone to lift.'

Cam hesitated and then said, 'It's great about the harp, dad. To tell you the truth, I'm jealous. Wish it had been me!'

His father grinned, his pride restored. Cam turned and started back up the field towards the house.

He had been going to go up to the plantation seeing he was up anyway, but the smell of breakfast from the kitchen was too much. He kicked off his boots and went in to where his mother was standing with the frying pan, basting the eggs with fat.

'Is that all for me?' he said with huge eyes and leant over her shoulder. She shook him off, but her eyes shone with pleasure at his teasing.

'I haven't seen you up this early since the days Rosie used to come for the eggs! What on earth have you been doing?'

'Dad'll tell you soon enough,' Cam said firmly and sat down at the table. Robert appeared in the doorway now, his dark hair tousled and his face puckered with sleep. He glowered at his brother.

'You made a noise like fifteen elephants going downstairs this morning. I could've murdered you.'

Cam smiled angelically. He had been the early bird just for once, and victory was sweet. His mother put a plate of sausage and eggs in front of him and he ate greedily, suddenly eager to be off on his own again. The first real sunlight burst through the kitchen

5

window and shone like silver over everything; he was thoroughly awake now and there was a restlessness in him like an ache. He would go up into the larch wood and then on. He wanted to use the day, to draw from it the last drop, and he was suddenly glad that his father had wakened him so early. He could hardly have borne to miss these first hours when everything was just starting to come to life.

He scraped back his chair.

'Thanks, Mum, that was great. I'm going out.' Already he was going out the door.

'Will you not even have some tea?' she called after him but he shouted back 'No thanks,' and was out into the bright magic of the light. The rain had gone off, and he looked away east, beyond the track and the plantation and the village to the low blue skies and the sun. His father was coming up from the field with strong, steady strides, and in his arms he carried the harp, as though it was a child he had found, a precious and beautiful child he was bringing home. Cam waved but he didn't see him; he was lost in his own world. The boy turned and began up towards the track that led into the larch wood.

The scent was what came to him first, that fresh, deep, green scent as the branches moved together under the breeze sounding like a great sea. The track now turned a corner and all of a sudden he was hidden by larches; the house, the sea and the fields were all swallowed up and no longer existed. Only the trees were left, chaffinches flitting away in small groups, and the sound of a pheasant whirring up into the air in its ungainly flight.

There was one place Cam wanted to go more than anywhere; had he remembered correctly, was it past the pool or did he go off to the right farther on? He stopped at the pond for a moment and looked at his reflection. Once he didn't have to bend at all to see the reflection of his face. Now he was nearly as tall as his father – and taller than Robert – something that did not please his brother one bit.

He bent down and put his hand into the water. It was like breaking black glass and the cold reached up to his wrist in sharp knives of pain. Over at the far side, the burn tumbled down into the pool the colour of crystal; it came from the moor and one of the hill lochs, finding its way through the deep carpet of larch

6

needles and quartz boulders to this place. Cam recalled the boats he used to sail here; he would spend hour after hour playing with them, pushing them round the rim of the pond, building islands of stones to which his ships voyaged to find treasure. He had made up his own stories, a world of legends, and narrated them aloud just as long as neither Robert nor any of his friends were within earshot. Once a few of them had hidden in the larches to watch him; they had burst out laughing at one of his stories. Mortified, he had pounded down the path to the house with hot tears on his face, buried himself in a pillow and refused to be comforted.

A group of pigeons flew from the treetops and Cam looked up, his thoughts forgotten. He had been wanting to find the glade anyway; he hadn't meant to stop there at all. He walked now on a thick carpet of moss, feeling tiny edges of damp seep through his shoes, for all the ground by the pool was black and wet. It took him longer than he expected to find the glade, but he broke in there at last, and stopped, breathing hard, squinting up at the sunlight as it strummed down in arrows through the thick green boughs. They were like the strings of the harp, he thought. He recalled what had once happened to him here…had it been real or just something he had wished would happen? He couldn't even recall how old he had been…

His mother had been in the habit of reading tales of Scottish history to Robert and himself – stories of Border warfare, of cattle rustled and prisoners set free, of battles for keeps and castles. She read them when the curtains were drawn and they were cosy in their beds, and he would lie awake long after the light had gone out, wishing he could have known those days.

One morning – it was probably a Saturday – he had wandered up into the larch wood, most likely on his way to his grandparents' place, when he was waylaid by the sight of a deer; he turned aside and went crashing through the larches after it, to find himself suddenly in that strange glade, timeless in its silence, the finches fluttering about in the held breath of the air. He half-remembered lying down there to look up at the canopy of the branches and the way the sun was spliced by the larches, when there came a sudden drumming, the echo of strong hooves, and the passing of that great black horse with its rider, a flag in his armoured hand, his head bent as he galloped on without a glance to left or right.

It was as though he had been in a nowhere place, as though all sorts of curtains of time had rushed together to allow him to see through, into something that had happened long, long before. Somehow he had been aware that the rider had been a messenger, that he was coming from a battle; but Cam had never bothered to find out more, to look up any book that would have helped him to identify the rider and place him in his context and time. Half of him kept the memory of that strange happening; perhaps the other half did not want to find out.

But today there was nothing, just the sound of the wind among the branches; he felt strangely disappointed by the place. It was not as he had imagined it, not as his memory wanted it to be. That thought almost frightened him – would he perhaps remember everything, when he was in Aberdeen, as his mind painted it, and then come back expectantly only to find an illusion?

Abruptly, he turned away, going back among the larches and letting the soft green boughs with their rain-wet edges brush across his face. The rain was back again now and he stopped by the pond, arguing with himself as to whether or not he should turn back. His bed wouldn't be really cold yet; it was a strong temptation. He decided to give the skies a chance; if the rain cleared a bit he'd go on over the moor to his grandparents' place; if not he'd find his way back and make a start on his packing. The thought hit him like a sharp slap as he began circling the pool to go on through the wood. Up to now, his leaving had seemed vague and distant; now he had to think in terms of suitcases, fees, bus passes, rent. For a second he had a vision of Union Street, with many feet going past and buses rushing as the same rain fell on the grey stone of the pavements.

If only, if only Richard were going! His eyes hurt with the thought. Richard, the best friend he had ever had; if he could only come back! But he was gone, and only the wind came like the touch of a hand on his cheek. Cam did not allow himself to cry.

All of a sudden he was out on the other side of the wood. Four grouse went bubbling away and he couldn't resist lifting an imaginary gun to his shoulder whilst making bangs with his mouth. Robert wouldn't have let them off so lightly, he reflected; he had an eye like a merlin's and a rock-steady hand. The number of dead things that had come home from that moor! Robert wasn't interested in them once they were dead, either, it was just the shooting of them that seemed to matter to him.

Cam looked up and over the moor. There, a little over to his left and far off, was the strange pyramid shape of Ben Luan, its sides of steeply-angled scree. His eye travelled round from the sea and the Ben, over the moor, to an old track that wound its way indistinctly over the heather, and then became lost. His heart lifted. That was the way to his grandfather's place. Before he left for Aberdeen he was going there. He had to say goodbye to its ghosts.

Between Ben Luan and the track was a long, low, dark line along the brow of the hill. That was where Cameron Mackay, the grandfather after whom he was named, used to cut his peats every summer. Cam screwed up his eyes and looked through the steady drizzle at the place; he saw the shadow clearly enough, bent over the peat cutter, methodically, patiently measuring out the next piece from the bank as the cutter went down and his left foot pressed it home. Cam could almost hear the thud of the peat as it was laid perfectly on the bank, ready to be stacked now in readiness for the long course of the winter. He saw himself, half the height he was now, running up through the larches with a flask for his grandpa, saw the old man turn, lean on the cutter and wave. He was always singing some Gaelic song or other to himself, humming away cheerily and singing so quietly that you couldn't catch the words. It was like getting a station on the radio when it was bad weather so that the voice is frayed and drifts away and you have to keep your ear close to hear it. That was how the songs had been; that was how his grandfather was now – just a station he occasionally found by chance, and remembered, and tried to listen to again.

Cam thought then of the peat bank and of the harp. It seemed to him that it was like that with memories; you went through layer and layer of them, back to the very beginning, and in the end you sometimes couldn't be sure what was a memory and what was a story. They could be either. He felt himself cutting away at the years, sifting through each place for the people and the stories. And in that peat there were harps and there were gemstones, and maybe knives and coffins as well; he wanted to find all of them, wanted to be sure.

But now it had turned again to rain in earnest and he didn't have

9

the heart to go on. Grey-black curtains had swept away Ben Luan and were smudging the peat bank and the old track.

Cam turned and started for home.

2

'Rosie's here for the eggs, Cam!'

He was already up and dressed; he'd been trying on different sweaters to make sure the blue lambswool was the best. It had one tiny hole in the left elbow, but if he pulled the sleeve round far enough... His hair was all flat now; he'd combed it in five different ways before he was satisfied, and had gone into his parents' bedroom on quiet feet to help himself to some of his father's aftershave. His hands were trembling a bit and he'd been to the bathroom twice, and had even practised his smile in front of the mirror.

Now he went hurtling downstairs and his mother, having exchanged a word or two with Rosie, vanished into the kitchen, giving her son a knowing wink as she went.

'Both of you come in for lemonade and biscuits when you're done,' she said, and the door closed behind her. Fleet snuffled and lay down.

'Hi,' Cam said and felt his cheeks going on fire.

'Hi,' answered Rosie, and there she was, the gentle bob of her dark brown hair, the rowan of her cheeks, the big brown eyes that caught his heart and sank him every time he saw her. His heart was drumming in his chest and with every second that passed his legs were more like jelly.

'So, can I have some eggs?' she asked, and there was the slightest hint of a smile on her lips. He came to and fumbled with his boots, nearly losing his balance, and she laughed, not at him in an unkind way but just for its own sake and because he amused her. She was in the class above him and was taller than him, and she could run like a wild hare.

'Fleet, go in!' he commanded in an uncommonly severe voice

which somehow restored his self-confidence. 'I'm only just up,' he muttered, moving off towards the hen-house. 'I didn't realise the time.' Then after a small silence, 'Richard and I are going for chestnuts tomorrow.'

Her eyes lit up.

'Aw, are you? Lucky things!'

'You can come if you like.' There, he had said it; he had actually got out the words and his heart, which had been going like a blacksmith's hammer, went quieter, the worst over. Cam was gaining courage by the second; something was pumping round in his veins that made him almost dizzy, and he felt taller and stronger.

'Aye, we're going to get them off that big tree in Mr Fraser's garden – you know, the one behind the hall?'

'He'll kill you if he finds you!'

'Och, we'll be all right. We'll come round for you about seven.'

They went into the darkness of the hen-house. It smelled of straw and warm air and dung; one or two swallows flitted about in the rafters and the hens conversed in a low clucking, for all the world, Cam thought, like ladies over their tea at the Women's Guild. It took them a moment or two to get used to the dark; he moved quickly and brushed his hand against hers, and for a moment their eyes met and he muttered 'sorry' and blundered away. The eggs in the nesting boxes were still warm, one or two of the shells slightly blotched with green dung, and they squeaked as he placed them carefully into the polystyrene box that Rosie had brought. His hands were trembling; he simply could not help it.

'Will you be a farmer one day, Cam?' she asked gently, and she was completely calm as she looked at him. He was taken aback and did not know how to answer; he was only just fourteen and he'd hardly thought yet.

'Robert'll get the farm,' he said automatically, for that was what he always heard his parents say. He put the sixth egg into the box and tried to close it tight. 'Maybe I'll go exploring in Africa.' Then it flashed across his mind that he was excluding her from his plans and he back-tracked hastily. 'Course I want to come back and live here. Wherever I go, it'll only be for a while.' He climbed down and gave her the box and she thanked him. 'What do you want to do yourself, Rosie?'

'I want to be a designer,' she answered, and there was real

feeling in her voice. 'I want to be really rich and go all round the world.'

He nodded, not knowing how to reply. It was as if she was a princess and miles above him; he looked down at his grubby hands and his confidence left him altogether. A kind of bubble rose up within him, his heart began to hammer again and he wanted...he knew he had to say it, now or never again.

'I'd be really sad if you went away. I really like you, Rosie.' And madly, wildly, he bent in a storm of feeling and kissed her cheek, except that he missed and got instead the lock of hair that came down about her ear. He was so dizzy he felt almost faint, and yet there was a wild elation in him too because he'd done it, he'd found the courage in the end.

She smiled at him and her voice was soft, not much more than a whisper.

'I like you too, Cam.'

He was standing at the window that evening, on the same day his father had found the harp, remembering Rosie, wondering about all that had happened since the day she came for the eggs. At first it wasn't clear in his mind at all; whole years of Saturdays seemed to have run into one. He realised nothing was left even to prove to himself the strong imprint she had left – no letter, no gift, no picture, not even a Valentine card. He looked out to the water and saw the tide far, far out, the shore grey and bleak in the foreground, and somehow the two things seemed the same to him; and yet she was like a flower growing deep down in some place in his mind. She had been his first love, and at the time she had meant everything to him.

He opened the window wide, lifting it so that he could lean right out into the early evening. There was a beautiful scent in the air; he did not know what it was. The low sun was weaker now, weak enough to look on full, and it came in a buttery yellow across the fields and the moors, changing and shifting, as elusive as a running child or a summer butterfly, searching and searching without ever coming to rest. He could hear the curlews again from down near the shore, though he could not see them, and he watched four oystercatchers fly over the shingle with their fast wingbeat, as if escaping from an enemy. Sometimes, when he was like this, intent on all the beauty about him, he knew that he feared death; he wanted never to lose hold of all this that was so precious to him. And because of all the memories of Rosie that had flooded into his mind again that day, at that moment he wanted her to be there too, for she was part of that world.

His mind would not stop thinking of her now – had they ever got the conkers that day? He thought hard. Now he remembered; Rosie hadn't come with them in the end, but Richard had fallen off the wall, and then a light had gone on in Mr Fraser's house and they had crouched down, hardly daring to breathe, until at last the light went off again and they had packed every pocket with beautiful chestnuts, polished so that they looked like mahogany.

After that, Cam remembered with a pang, he had neglected Richard badly. He had held Rosie's hand and she had written his name on her jotter with a red felt-tip pen; and every Saturday she came for a longer and longer time. She had helped him build the last of the den up in the larch wood and they talked there about a million things. They played tricks on his big brother; they put a frog in his bed and seaweed in his wellington boots. They went up into the loft of Ardnish house when it was raining, and opened up old trunks and played endless dressing-up games. And they had had some terrible arguments too; most of the time they were best friends but when they argued they did it in style. He had no idea now what it was they disagreed about. Sometimes Rosie would get very angry; she kicked things, and she nipped him. Once or twice, he remembered, he had kicked her too and that had made things much worse. It was usually Cam who said sorry first, very, very reluctantly, but he always had to drag any apology out of her. All the same, they never seemed to stay angry for long.

But then, one holiday time, everything fell apart for good. Cam's cousin, Beckie, who lived in Campbeltown, came to stay just after Christmas. The snow had come at last and there was enough in front of the house to get the sledges out and spin down all the way to the burn. Cam had shaken Beckie's hand rather icily when she first arrived; he had played compulsory games with her and then tried to sneak away as often as he could. She had freckles and glasses, and she liked maths at school, which made her, in Cam's eyes, a monstrous kind of figure, quite beyond the pale.

Then they went sledging. He found she was absolutely fearless; she would go backwards on the sledge, or she would stand on it and hurtle down the most terrifyingly steep inclines. Cam was quite bowled over; he forgot his cool front and became excited as a puppy with her, bounding about as he chatted.

'Aw, you should see the hill above the manse! It's miles long and if you get up a really good speed you go right over a bump at the bottom and straight over a fence! It's really scary but you'd love it, I'm telling you!'

That was the Saturday, the last one before they went back to school. Rosie was puzzled that she hadn't heard anything from him that morning, so she bumped along the farm track with her sledge, all muffled up in her winter gear. She came round the back of the farm just as Cam and Beckie had toppled over together in the middle of the top field and were lying in a heap, roaring their heads off and nearly crying with laughter. Rosie looked from one to the other and in an instant made up her mind as to what was going on. Her face crimson, she shouted at the top of her voice 'I hate you, Cam Mackay! I don't want to see you ever again!' And she stamped away as he sat there looking at her with his mouth half open, and new flakes of snow twirled out of the heavy, grey skies. Three days later Beckie was away on the train and school had begun. The snow had melted, and the pool of ice under the pear tree had gone, but Rosie walked past Cam as tall and frigid as an icicle. Worst of all, she chose to sit beside the boy he most detested in his class, Mitchell Simpson, and shared his lunch. He watched them in anguish. His whole world seemed to have collapsed. He pushed his food around his plate and seemed hardly to hear when anyone asked him a question. His mother watched him quietly, not knowing how to help; she said nothing when Calum, Rosie's brother, came the following Saturday for the eggs. Cam was still in bed.

After the boy had left, she crept upstairs and stood in a pool of morning sunlight, holding her breath as she listened outside her younger son's door. He had been crying so long that he hardly had the breath to sob any more; his red face was buried in the pillow. He felt desolate and completely confused, above all angry with himself for having lost her. He told himself that he would never, never fall in love with anyone in his life again, but remain distant and lonely and full of bitterness. He sobbed heavily again and then turned to face the wall as his mother came very quietly into the room and closed the door. He had known she would come but he didn't turn round, and buried his face in the pillow again.

'Cam?' she said softly and sat on the edge of the bed. 'Cam, I think I know why you're so upset, and I just wanted you to know that I understand.'

He moaned in frustration. There was nobody in the world who could understand! His mother thought of taking his hand but then thought better of it. Cam was growing up and maybe it would remind him even more of Rosie.

'I'll go if you really want me to,' she said then, 'but I thought you might like to hear a story. Would that be all right?'

In reply he gave a kind of whimper which she couldn't translate, but she decided to stay anyway. Afterwards she would cook sausages for his dinner, and invite Richard over as a surprise.

'There was once a man who lived in a Highland glen,' she began, 'away up in the very far north of Scotland, in Sutherland. He had a hard life all right, cutting enough peats to see him through the winter, and getting milk and cheese from his two cows. He was always very lonely during the bad weather, for it blew like a hurricane from October till February and at times it was nearly impossible to walk a step on the road outside his door. Now and again his nearest neighbours, who lived maybe three miles away, would send word that they were going to have a ceilidh, and he would excitedly get down his old fiddle from the wall and march along the road, no matter what the weather was like, and they would have songs and a lot of good talk, and sometimes a dram as well, and plenty of oatcakes and cheese.

'Well, one night when he went to their house there was a girl there who was the most beautiful girl you could possibly imagine. She had long golden hair and eyes that were the colour of moorland lochs, a kind of deep blue-black. She laughed and she danced, and when she smiled at the man it seemed to burn into his very heart. He found out from his friends that she had come to look after an old relative who couldn't manage on her own any more, and when he heard that the man's heart began to beat very fast, for he wanted so much to see her again.

'But then his heart failed him because she was so beautiful and everyone seemed to like her, so how could he possibly believe she would ever look at him? So he did nothing, and the spring passed and then the summer came, and he was miserable because he didn't know what to do. Soon she might go away again and he'd have lost his chance!

'So one night he plucked up courage and asked if he could keep her company on the way home from the ceilidh, and she agreed. And as they stood outside her door he said shyly the thing he'd wanted to say for so long.

"I know that I love you. Would you…could you ever be my wife?"

'But she just laughed and then held his hand lightly in hers and looked away over the land, and her eyes as he looked at her seemed to be filled with the stars. And then she said quietly that she did not yet know what it was she wanted, that she needed time to think it all over. Then the door closed and she was gone, and he was left alone in the dark emptiness of the night.

'Day after day he waited, hoping against hope for an answer, but she never came to the house. Then again there was a ceilidh, and every man there wanted to dance with her and it seemed to the man that she was like a kind of golden sun among them all. Once more the faithful man guided her home and dared to ask her again if she had thought about his question and if she had an answer for him.

"Oh, I will think about it, I really will," she answered. "There's been so much in my mind lately, I never have had time, but I will, I promise."

'So he took her at her word and once more he waited; he waited right through the long winter. But still there was no sign of her as the snow ran off the hills and the first lambs began to appear in the fields. Several times more after that he asked her, until after one ceilidh that went on and on until after the dawn she stood on the doorstep and laughed and said: "When you've made me a wedding ring from the gold that's in the river, then I'll promise to marry you."

'She did not really think what she was saying; the words did not mean a thing to her, for she was too happy with all the men around to want any of them at all. But the farmer believed that this was a real test she was setting him, and he went out at dawn the very next morning and began panning the river for gold. He dug down deep into the silt and found tiny winks of gold, thin as paper, left in the bottom of his pan. Each piece he kept with the utmost care; sometimes he would find slightly bigger pieces, so that the time came when there was almost enough. He was so desperate to win the girl he loved that he neglected the work of his own farm and spent every minute of his time searching the river pools. At last he melted what he had into one lump and knew then that he needed only one tiny nugget for the work to be done.

'So, one day of snow and gale, he went out again to search. He felt sick with the cold and soon he was drenched with the blizzard, but still he kept on. On the afternoon of that day he found the last precious piece he needed; later the ring was made. That very night he trudged through the snow to her house and knelt at her feet to offer the ring she had asked for. Her face turned white as ash.

"But I never meant you to do it!" she cried. "I need more time; I need to think! And I really will, I promise."

'But the poor man was broken. He rose up from where he was kneeling on the stone, and he did not say a word. He knew now that she could never love him, and he turned and went away, as pale as a ghost. And they say that soon afterwards he died, for his heart had been broken.'

Gradually Cam had come to listen. By the end, he had his head on his elbows while he stared out through the window, not saying a word. His mother smiled as she finished, and dared to take his hand and squeeze it.

'It's a hard road you have to travel,' she said after a silence. 'But one day you'll find the right one, and just don't go and make wedding rings till you're sure they'll keep them.'

In spite of himself, he smiled – at least, his mouth twitched and he turned away, because he didn't want to look happy too quickly.

'It's just that Rosie misunderstood,' he said sorrowfully, and then found himself blurting the whole thing out. 'She saw Beckie and me together in the snow and thought we were going out together and I was two-timing her!'

Cam's face puckered again and he cried as if his heart would break, for the loss of Rosie, for the poor man and his ring, for the hopelessness of everything. He let his mother gather him into her arms and he soaked her shoulder...

But all that had been years ago. Now they were older; it was all water under the bridge. Cam was still standing by the window, in the same room where he had cried his eyes out for Rosie, and it made him feel strange to think about it. He could never tell her,

17

not even now, not as something to laugh about. Too much pain was still in the memory. Oh, he had picked himself up all right, and by the time that spring's lambing was over he had almost forgotten the snow and Beckie and all the trouble she had caused. Rosie's winter passed too, and by the summer her frosty mood had melted enough for her to say hello to him, very carefully and quietly. Mitchell Simpson had abandoned her long ago and was at least three girls farther on, and maybe she was beginning to miss the old days herself. But her pride had been so hurt that day in December that she could not allow herself to forget. She saw well enough that when Cam walked near her he went like a wounded fawn, but she wanted him to suffer; she wanted him to know the pain she had been through. One day she might let the walls come down, but not yet…

Where was she going now? Oh yes, somewhere in Edinburgh, a management course in one of the colleges – a far cry, he thought, from her old dreams of fashion designing in London! She had a boyfriend in Fort William who came every weekend on a wasp of a motorbike; she smoked now and was much louder, and like most of them couldn't wait to get away to the city, away from 'this boring place'. Somehow he wished he could go back in time, back to that first time he'd met her at the door, on the day she had come for the eggs. Maybe he could have made everything different, if Beckie hadn't come, and they had stayed together. But what was the use of thinking like that? It was too late to change anything now.

The sun poured down over the sea in a shining circle and it was like a golden ring, a ring you could never catch. If you took a boat out from the shore you could paddle for all your worth and never get there, never reach that magical ring.

He would meet a sea of girls in Aberdeen. He smiled to himself and imagined for a moment – in a few days he would be there! But afterwards the experience would be tarnished, and he didn't want that either. But maybe his mother had been right, and there would be one who would take his gold forever? He didn't know. It lay in the sun coming up tomorrow and although he wanted to know the answer, it somehow excited him that he didn't; thinking of it now was like hundreds of butterflies in his heart.

Tomorrow, he decided, he would go to the croft. It would be a lovely day tomorrow, and that was exactly where he wanted to go. A picture of his grandfather flashed across his mind. If only he had seen the harp. If only he'd lived to see it!

3

As Cam went across the moor, struggling against the tug of the wind and the driving rain (his weather predictions had been completely wrong) he heard the raven's deep croak. It was a sound made out of coal; the raven itself was made of coal. He stopped walking and looked all around intently; the cronking gave him a strange prickly feeling down his spine. There they were, just one pair of them on the moor; there was nothing else at all to be seen between them and Ben Luan, nothing but the mist. Then the ravens went over a rocky knoll and were lost to view. Cam was alone now, and he felt the better for it.

He was following the ancient track to his grandfather's croft, and the big metal key to its door was in his pocket. He had been half-reluctant to leave because of the rain, and his mother had fussed over him, insisting that he take this and that before he went. With Robert in a bad mood and his father annoyed at having to fill in a lot of forms he had been glad enough to leave the house.

'I'll try to be back in time for dinner but don't worry about me if I'm not,' he told his mother. 'I've known the road since I could walk, remember!'

Now he felt bad that he'd been impatient with his mother. She always got caught in the middle when he and Robert fell out with each other, or when his father was annoyed about something. Anyway he was sick of the constant rows with his brother; Robert hadn't even looked at him when he had passed the shed where he was working.

Now the rain was getting heavier. He looked back and saw that Ardnish was completely blotted out, and so was the sea. Now and again bits of Ben Luan loomed out of the mist, making it seem as if a huge pyramid was there, towering over the plateau. He began to think of the First World War, in which his grandfather had fought, and he found himself wondering whether the two landscapes might have seemed to him quite similar; the land was pock-marked by craters which you could imagine had been made by shells; with a stretch of imagination you could make yourself believe the mist over the promontories was enemy gas. Cam could even see a ragged line of grey men coming from behind a ditch and then being lost in the mist. He pulled himself together and laughed at himself for being so fanciful.

The track was now gone. He had to stop and look about him, frowning, to make sure he was heading in the right direction. Where was the single pine tree? As a wee boy, that was the thing he had always looked forward to, the one tree in all that emptiness, its branches all keeled over to the east, flattened so that it looked like a man being beaten and cowering under the whip. He really needed that landmark, for on such a day as this you could have wandered on for ten miles and more through the mist, only to find yourself hopelessly lost.

Toberdubh. The place where his grandfather had lived all on his own after his wife died. She had gone suddenly, the summer before Cam was born; a stroke had taken away her speech, they told him, as well as the power from her left side. Before that she had been as strong and busy as a woman thirty years younger. But after the stroke Peggy fell away to nothing; she became gentle and she cried a lot, and she had no will to live at all. In that way, they said, it was a blessing she had died; that was what Duncan, Cam's father, said himself.

After that, somehow, Cameron Mackay had gone on living at Toberdubh alone. Cam thought about it now and wondered how he had ever managed to do it. His mind went back to his very first memories of the place; they were in black and white, and fragmentary. When, for instance, had he tasted whisky? He remembered the smell from the glass, the hot burning taste. It had put him off the stuff for life!

Now memories came crowding back. It was before he'd begun at school, or maybe during his first year at primary; he wasn't sure. Anyway, he had gone out to see his grandpa and it had rained in rods all day. He'd gone running to his favourite place on the ridge above Toberdubh, a peat-bank where he could hide in under the walls and pretend it was his own house. It was beginning to get dark when he heard his grandfather shouting for him, and he scrambled out of the peat-bank, which was filled with mud like chocolate, to see the single yellow light above the back door of Toberdubh and his grandfather in the doorway. The rain was heavier than ever and Cam bolted like a rabbit down the heathery ridge, his mind full of thoughts of tea and the fire, when down he went into a bog. He gasped for breath, utterly taken by surprise and up to his neck in black mud.

'You'll be out in a minute,' old Cameron chuckled. 'That'll teach you to run like a train down the hill! You'll have to learn to look where you're going, boy!'

Cam remembered bursting into angry tears; he was cold, covered in black clammy peat, and shivering. Suddenly he wanted to be back at Ardnish with his mother more than anything in the world.

'Wheesht, laddie! You'll be home soon, never fear. Now, a nice hot bath and a wee tot of whisky and you'll be as right as rain again, you'll see.'

The bath was good, right enough, and Cam enjoyed lying in comfort listening to the rain and wind hammering on the window, but he was still a bit sorry for himself. So his grandfather wrapped him in a massive towel and carried him downstairs and sat him down beside a roaring fire. Old Balach the collie was banished to a corner, and then a small glass was put into Cam's hand, with just a thimbleful of gold liquid which caught the reflection of the flames.

'Go on now,' said the old man. 'You won't like it, I know, but it'll keep you from catching cold.'

Cam put his nose into the glass and then sneezed violently. He looked quizzically up at his grandfather who was shaking with mirth; at last, to please him, he ventured to take a sip. Immediately he started to cough; he made a face and spluttered: 'It tastes awful!' Nothing would make him take anther drop after that.

'Och well, I think I'll tell you a story,' old Cameron said then, 'and I hope you'll remember it well. Then you can be off to your bed and you'll sleep like a top. It's a story of how the devil first got the taste of whisky.

'Now the devil lives in a horrible deep den, away far down inside the earth, right at the very centre where everything is on fire and it's just fearfully hot, like an oven. Well, a long, long time ago he was sitting down there when this strange smell came into his nose and he couldn't think what it was or where it was coming

21

from. In the end he was sure it was coming from the earth above him and so he came bursting up through all his dark dens and caves until at last he reached the place where the smell was coming from. He wandered around for a while; it was cold and wet and miserable. And then who should come out of his hut, playing his bagpipes, but a man called Fraser Campbell. He got the most fearful fright when he saw the devil and ran back into the hut and slammed the door, but the devil soon got in; he knew fine it was from there that the wonderful smell was coming. Inside was a whole array of bubbling glass bottles and tubes, filled with this strange yellowy-gold liquid, and on the table stood a glass full of the stuff. Without even asking he went over and drank it, and it warmed him up all through. So he took away as many bottles as he could carry, and off he went. The man was glad to get rid of him, but it wasn't for long – every now and again he was back for more, and there was nothing he could do about it.'

Cam was half-asleep by the time the story was finished, but he had completely forgotten about the bog and the cold, and how miserable he was. He remembered his grandfather picking him up and carrying him upstairs to bed, but he was asleep by the time they reached the top of the stairs.

Every time he even sniffed whisky he still recalled that night long ago, and the weird story his grandfather had told him – strange, he now thought, that the old man should have told him a story like that. But in their family stories always played an important part, especially for taking your mind off things that were troubling you. So his thoughts ran, recalling old memories of this place, until he stopped in his tracks and his eyes burned as he found himself looking down again at Toberdubh from the ridge. Even now he missed the heathery grey tuft of smoke fluttering from the old chimney. In the old days, he thought, one of the dogs would have been up by now from the fireside and out to the door, barking away at the scent of the approaching visitor, and his grandpa scolding it for making such a noise, as he tramped out toward the back door. At one time, the walls had been as white as scrubbed clam shells; now there were big damp patches stretching down from the roof, and loose slates clacked in the wind. For a few moments he just stood there, looking down at the old house; it seemed to him that it was itself a ghostly thing, filled with the sadness of departed spirits. It was like going to tend a grave; this was the real place where his grandparents were buried rather than the graveyard down by the church! But the rain had come on harder than ever and pulling himself together, he began to slither down the steep bank and reached the back door at a half run. He searched for the big key and let himself in.

Something fell from the shelf in front of him and made a ringing noise as it rolled across the floor – a candle, still in its enamel holder. He went into the sitting-room and it was gloomy, cast into shadow by the dark of the afternoon outside; the wind seemed to roll about the house, tugging at its foundations so violently that the place felt a bit like a boat whose anchor was straining to keep hold of it. The house was still furnished, for now and again Cam's father let the place to folk as a summer cottage, or to shooting parties in the autumn. The trouble was, as always, that whenever Cam came here he saw his grandfather wherever he turned; if he looked outside, he could see him working on the walls, or maybe digging in the overgrown garden, or inside he would be kneeling by the fire, making a good blaze.

Why had he come back? Why was he here now, putting himself through this torment when nothing in the world would bring the old man back? He thought about it as he searched around for some kindlings to light the fire. He found himself wishing that his grandfather had known he'd got the place at Aberdeen.

'You stick in at your lessons now, boy! You've a good head on you, Cam.' His grandpa had known, of course, that Rob would be the one to take over Ardnish in the fullness of time. There wasn't enough work for the two brothers to share the place, so Cam had always known he'd have to make his own way somewhere else. No-one had ever actually talked about it; it was just something that was understood and taken for granted in the family. Often the old man would come back to the subject, asking him if he'd thought what he wanted to be, maybe a doctor or an engineer? 'I don't know,' Cam had replied with some irritation one time. 'I've no idea what I'll do. I've plenty time to choose yet.'

'Aye, but see you stick in at your work, Cam. You don't get many second chances in this life, you know, and you may regret it...'

'I'm sick of grandpa going on at me about my school work,' Cam remembered complaining one night at Ardnish. 'He goes on about it the whole time. I wish he'd give me some peace! Can you not tell him to leave me for a bit, dad?'

'Come here and listen.' His father's voice was gentle but strong. He was wearing his glasses as he sat there at the kitchen table, accounts and forms spread round him like autumn leaves. 'When your grandfather came back from the war his nerves were shattered; he couldn't concentrate on a thing. He'd been brilliant at maths and science and he never got a chance to use them. When he got back here all he could do was work the croft, and by the time he had got a bit better he had a family on his hands – no chance of university for him in those days! And Cam, try to understand – he's only human, and maybe he's just a little jealous. Wouldn't you be, if you were him?'

That was all. His dad had turned back then to his work and never said another word. Cam felt his cheeks flame with guilt. He went over to the window and looked out at the last of the sun, and saw away over the moor a faint trail of smoke that might be from Toberdubh. Fool that he'd been, he thought now; he'd just taken it for granted that the croft was all his grandfather had ever wanted. Next time he'd remember, and be more understanding.

He couldn't help thinking of it all again years later, back here at the old house, kneeling by the grate to get the fire going. How proud the old man would have been to know of his place at Aberdeen! Suddenly he had a picture of himself running over the moors to Toberdubh with the piece of paper in his hand, desperate to tell the old man his news as he always did when anything exciting happened. There would have been a celebration, and certainly a dram!

When the first flames rose and lit the hearth they somehow threw the room into greater darkness. Cam got up, went to find the power switch and flicked on a light. He returned to the sitting-room and there, for just a moment, he fancied he was the old man stretched out on the couch, his eyes on him, the white hair splayed out behind his head.

'I got the place,' Cam whispered to him. 'I'm going to Aberdeen, but I'll be back! I'd never go away for good.' Then it seemed that the blue eyes were lit, and he smiled as he said: 'Mind you stick in when you're there, then'. But the couch was empty again, and the wind came round the house howling like wolves, and the boy shivered.

Now he became uneasy; he recalled what old Cameron had told him of the strange light that appeared on the shoulder of Ben Luan. It was not a bright light at all, and it didn't keep to the one place; nor was it that all the folk in a village like Findale would see it at the one time, but it would appear to one here and there, as though it shone only in their direction. There was old Murdo Fraser who had gone out in the night from Crossallan, determined to search out this mysterious thing, not sure if it was perhaps some poor soul who'd gone up to climb the hill and been benighted there. At any rate, his grandfather said, he was back by morning, weak and weary, having found not a thing – he lost the light after wandering for a while over the screes and got nothing but a cold for his pains. And when the lambing snow came a couple of weeks later, Murdo was dead and gone.

Chrissie Bain had seen the thing too, according to the old man, not many weeks before she passed away. Oh, there had been plenty... By now Cam had got himself really frightened; all of this was like a kind of marsh in his mind over which he was afraid to tread. He was thirsty, and he wanted to brew up some tea, but he had become like a child again, frightened of the unknown thing that might be round the corner. What if he, when he looked out of the window, should catch a glimpse of the eerie light? What if his own grandfather had seen it just before he died? By now Cam's heart was hammering in his chest and he was becoming so afraid that he didn't even want to move... He should go home, he should go home! But the rain and the wind were blattering on the windows and roof so fiercely that he dared not set out with the feeble little torch which was all he had. He would have to wait until morning, when he could find his way without any trouble.

When the outer door opened suddenly he nearly died of fright; he leapt up, his heart hammering. It was his father who came into the room, a strong torch still lit in his hands.

'Aye, you picked the night for coming here all right! Your mother said you'd no torch and she wouldn't rest till I came to get you.'

Why did she never stop fussing? Wouldn't she ever allow him to grow up? These were his first impatient thoughts. In a moment his foolish fears were gone, the other, fearful world at once shut out. He got up and filled the kettle, saying in casual tones to his father, 'Thanks for coming, dad. I'd have been fine. I was going to stay over and come back in daylight.' His father hardly heard him; he was checking cupboards and running his hands over the walls.

'The place is still in fairly good shape. The Fothergills or whatever their name was have left things pretty well. Just a mug of tea then, Cam, and we'd better be off. I've a pile of things to attend to before I get to bed.'

That was all. So that was all this place was to him – a letting house for holidays! He, Cam, couldn't go round the back without seeing the old, dry ruins of the well and imagining an old bent back working at lifting a bucket of water; he couldn't stand by the door without remembering the black beehive of peat that used to stand there against all the winds of winter, every turf made of effort and life. He wanted to turn to his father and look him straight in the eyes and ask if he didn't feel the presence of the old man here yet – was he so soon forgotten? Was a life so easily scrubbed out and lost, washed away by a strong river, leaving no trace? Maybe his father did remember...maybe he had just become too good at hiding it.

They walked home together through the wild night, hardly talking; the silence between them was comfortable. In places the track was under water; streams ran off the slopes that rose towards Ben Luan, showing white even in the darkness. Now Cam felt strong, unafraid of his grandfather's eerie tales; he looked across towards the Ben and inwardly challenged it to show any light, but there was nothing, nothing in all the wide expanse except the nodding beam of his father's torch, nothing to be heard but the wind, and the heavy thud of their boots as they trudged on towards Ardnish. In the end Cam reached the point where he marched without thinking; he no longer felt the ache of his calves or the cold of his fingertips after the unceasing, drenching rain. His feet led him but his spirit was far away.

He thought of his grandfather's last days and how quickly the old man had faded in the end. There had been so little warning of the final fall that it came as a shock to jolt them all, and even sent tremors through Findale and far beyond. It was as though a stout ship that had had no accident all its days had suddenly gone on to the rocks, to be wrecked within hours. That last summer old Cameron had still brought in the peats to Toberdubh, although Rob had helped a good deal with the cutting and had done most of the stacking too. He had seemed much the same as ever – maybe a bit more stubborn and at times quick to flare up. But then he fell. He went over on his ankle and lay helpless half a day before one of the local shepherds passed by chance and managed to get him up to the house.

After that, his son Duncan made no bones about the fact that he was coming to Ardnish whether he liked it or not. He didn't like it, of course, and he came with bad grace, and was put into Cam's room. The two brothers had to share a room for the first time in years and agreed to it dourly, as suspicious of each other as a couple of strange sheepdogs.

But the old man went down very fast. Maybe it was a mistake to uproot him from the croft that had been his home ever since he married Peggy; it was the only world he knew. Ardnish was maybe too loud, and too young, and he felt out of joint there. The fall had twisted more than his ankle; in truth he had suffered a first stroke, and in no more than a handful of days he slipped from their grasp so quickly that they could only watch helplessly as the strong man went downhill and was soon lost to them for ever.

It was strange that during those final days he talked nothing but Gaelic; he wasn't really with them any more. On his face, Cam recalled, there was a kind of shining look of complete serenity. The strange thing was that when Duncan went the next day to Toberdubh he found a clock fallen from the mantelpiece; he couldn't understand how it had happened, but it seemed as though time itself had stopped.

Now they came to the larch wood and heard the whispering of the branches as drops of water fell among them and ran through the boughs. There seemed to be a strange kind of warmth in the trees after the open wildness of the moor. The two of them went quickly down the last yards towards the back door of the farmhouse. Rob's light was still on and cast a pale yellow reflection over the ground below; from behind the window came the sound of loud music and Rob's own voice singing along with it. Cam's mother was fussing about the kitchen, picking up nothings from beside the stove, as the two of them went in.

'You should have started back earlier, Cam,' she said accusingly, looking at him with sparking eyes. 'Your poor father...'

'Och, mum,' Cam said, going past her towards the far door. 'Can't you let me go? I'm not a child any more.'

He looked back at her as he opened the door to go up to his bedroom and their eyes met. He saw a sadness in her face that he had never seen before. For a moment he wanted to go back, to say he was sorry, and take away that loss from her eyes which he knew would haunt him; but he didn't. He shut the door and went heavily up to his room, and then opened his window and listened to the sea far off.

He would go down to Shuan, for Richard's sake. Not just yet, but certainly before he left. It was one thing he simply must do.

4

During the night Cam dreamed something that he was to remember for a long time after. He was restless in his sleep, waking first because the window was banging as the rain came in many fingertips across the glass. He saw the moon rushing through cloud like a silver coin, before he crashed back into bed, shivering with cold. He was thinking about his grandfather as he went back to sleep, soundly this time. In his dream, he was going over the moors in front of Ben Luan; at first Richard was with him and afterwards he was not. At any rate Cam found himself at the edge of a lochan that seemed to be covered in specks of white. At first he thought these were snowflakes, but as he drew nearer he realised they were water lilies, their heads half-closed as they bobbed on the surface of the water. He knew he must pick one at once, no matter how cold the water might be, no matter how deep; he was also aware that if he got one, Rosie would be his again – he would give the lily to her and she would be his forever. His clothes seemed in some magical way to flow from him and in a moment he was down into the black water, right up to his thighs. As he went deeper and deeper, the cold was worse than anything he could have imagined, like knives of steel through every fibre of his being. He could see clearly the very lily he wanted; it had a beautiful golden heart within its petal sheath. He stretched out for it with his fingertips; the water now rose up to his neck, the dark tendrils of the lilies beneath caught his legs making him flounder, dragging him down so that he could not breathe...

He woke up terrified, with the wind tapping at the glass like a teacher on a blackboard. For a second he was sure there was someone else in the room; he held his breath in fear, but then the wind was quiet and he dared to look up, and there was nothing except the moon splaying down brilliant milky light on to the floor. He recalled the dream in vivid detail but could not understand it; he had a strange feeling of somehow being at war with himself. He wondered why this should be; perhaps it was because recently Richard had been so much in his thoughts.

He saw that it was a quarter past six. Soon it would be time to get up; it was Saturday, and he had promised himself that he would begin his packing in earnest today. But he did not want to start. Fear gripped him from time to time that the whole thing was a dreadful mistake, that he was being a complete fool. Surely anything would be better than throwing away this place he loved so much – he could easily get a job in Findale instead; he could stay on at home... But it would not be as he dreamed of it now. That was the worst of both the future and the past – they were always pure and unspoiled. But in the end they did not really exist. Only now was real.

Suddenly he found himself wishing with all his heart that Richard was still there – to talk to, to argue with, to understand. He wanted him back, so badly that it hurt him physically, like cramp in his stomach. Richard was dead; Richard would never come back! Cam lay there in bed as the wind howled outside, hot and angry tears running down his face. Why, why did things have to be so hard? He felt like a child, lost and out on his own, reaching for the lily that he could never, never hold.

'Can I borrow that new shirt of yours? There's a party on at Camas tonight.'

Robert was already halfway inside his younger brother's wardrobe, searching for the precious shirt Cam had got last Christmas. He had wakened up with a start when Robert began talking, and he hauled himself round in the bed to see the time. Ten to ten! His head was heavy and still thudding with sleep. Robert had the shirt now and was taking it off the hanger. Cam got up furiously and snatched at it.

'I never said you could have it, right? At least have the decency to wait for an answer! I want it for Aberdeen next week so you can't have it tonight. Give it back!'

He was still tugging at the sleeve, half in and half out of bed, really rattled now by the way Rob had just barged in to help himself to what he wanted. He was only doing it to see how far he could push Cam; there was a kind of triumphant look on his face as he still kept hold of the shirt, scoffing, sure of his supremacy.

'What're you going to need this for next week, huh? All you're doing is studying. Might as well take your school blazer and uniform with you! You're too young even to be allowed in a pub.'

'Just give me back that shirt!' Cam realised he was whining, which made him madder than ever. The roles were as they always had been. The door opened abruptly and his mother put her head round.

'Rob, give it back to Cam! Your dad's wanting you to help him.'

Cam ripped it back with righteous indignation, still looking daggers at his brother. Rob went over to the door, grinning like a jackal.

'Cry baby,' he said scornfully over his shoulder as he left. Morag's eyes passed over Cam after Rob had gone out but she did not say anything. She had taken sides too often in the past and Cam had rebuffed her last night for interfering. The house was filled with the smell of fresh baking; her shoes clacked as she quickly descended the stairs. Cam still raged within himself. What a fool he had been to think he could ever stay on in this house! He hated his brother and couldn't wait to be free of him. He bashed his fist into the pillow and lay, face down and eyes closed, until he felt calmer, his turbulent thoughts quietened down. But he found he couldn't lie in bed any longer so he threw off the bedclothes, got up and looked out of the window. The fields shimmered with rain. Still, he had made up his mind to go to Shuan; later, perhaps, he would go.

He saw his mother at the far end of the kitchen as he went in. Her head was bent as she kneaded dough for bread. Silhouetted by a sudden ray of sunshine from the window, it might have been that she was praying. She had not heard him come in, and for a moment he stood quietly watching her, thinking of how he had distanced himself from her the night before. He allowed his gaze to wander around all the familiar things in the room; everything seemed to be black and gold in the light. Misty and Fruin lay stretched out like a couple of hearth-rugs; his father's boots stood drying after the soaking of the previous night.

A black ridge of cloud then passed over the sun and the room was plunged into shadow. Cam looked up at the long prow of cloud and it reminded him of something from childhood, a time when he had believed a strange hobgoblin rode such clouds as these. Sometimes he could actually see the high cape around the creature's shoulders and the outline of the black mount on which it galloped across the skies! And once, he recalled, he had been so frightened that he had run down from his room, scared that the hobgoblin was real.

'I'll do a final wash for you today, Cam.' His mother's voice interrupted his reverie. 'Bring anything you need done.'

Cam looked at her. She sounded tired, as though she hadn't slept well the night before. Most likely she had been up since six too. She turned and began to shape the dough.

'Thanks, Mum.' He said it as gently as he could, really meaning it and wanting to make amends. 'I dunno how I'm going to cope with everything on my own.'

She put down what she was doing and came over to him. 'Och, you'll be fine, Cam. No doubt you'll be home often enough with plenty washing!'

He wanted to tell her that he didn't even know that he wanted to go, that he was scared of leaving Ardnish and all that was familiar here for the first time ever, that he would miss her. But his mouth seemed dry and he didn't know where to begin, and his hands knotted helplessly on the wooden table; he simply stood looking at her as she now went round the kitchen gathering things to be washed.

There was always so little time in this house. Were other families like this? It was nobody's fault, but it was everyone's. They were always so busy doing their own things; they talked instead of listening. When they were children, he and Rob had talked to their mother much more; then, there was no fear of embarrassment, of being seen to be weak and foolish. He wondered how long it was since all that had changed. Now the room was back to silence and he didn't know how to begin. It was as if he held many broken pieces in his hands and he did not know which one to bring out first. Angry with himself, he turned and went up the stairs to the attic without having spoken another word.

He thought of how often he had raced up the steep stairs, two steps at a time, the echoes sounding round the house as Richard or some other friend came after him. The place had a low ceiling, and set into the sloping roof were two small windows that looked east. Cam went over to one of them, still breathing hard after having run so fast, and down and away to the right he could see the grey smudge of Findale, the church steeple poking the sky like a needle, the hills and woods beyond. The mist had almost gone; the last of it was like thin stretches of wool, drawn now over the low ground around the river.

He dragged himself away from the window and forced himself to think of his packing. He had come up for a trunk, to take all that he would need for his first term, but he had no heart for it; he simply had no wish to start. His eyes grew accustomed to the dim light; there was dust over everything. At one time, he remembered, he and Robert would be up here every single day; whenever there was rain, their adventures automatically moved in from the fields and the shore to this secret place. Cam spotted something metal shining on the floor and bent to pick it up. It was a Redcoat soldier firing his musket. He smiled, remembering how at one time their war games had stretched from one end of the attic to the other, and how the battles had gone on for days. Cam looked at the soldier and turned it in his hands. The war games had ended a long time ago; it was real conflicts with Robert that went on now! A sadness fell across him for a moment and he let the little soldier fall. What was the point of it all in the end?

As a child he had loved nothing more than rummaging through old boxes or trunks, that had maybe come from Toberdubh, or from an old uncle who had been a ship's captain and had sailed round the world. There was always the hope in him that he'd find something really precious, perhaps a gold coin that had been passed over, or an ancient letter unread for centuries. He picked out an old tin box, easily side-tracked both by memories of past joys and the desire to stay up there out of Robert's way, and in a place where there was complete peace.

He didn't find much in it. This was one of the boxes he had stowed away years ago, full of things he'd been made to clear out from his bedroom. There was an old rusted bit of metal he'd once dug up in a field which he'd been quite sure was Roman; an assortment of shells that had come from a white eternity of beach on the Island of Harris; various old buttons of odd shapes and sizes with which he had played for hours on end when he was small. At the back of his mind, though, as he sifted through the collection of junk, was the hope that he might come across something given to him by Rosie. She was gone now, of course, and he had no thought or hope of regaining her, yet the memory of her was still inside him, part of all the memories of this place, and somehow he didn't want to forget. But there was nothing.

Then, from the bottom of the box, he dragged out a scruffy white feather; as he twirled it in his hands he realised that it was a quill. Somehow it touched off an old memory; he set his mind to thinking hard what it was, and gradually it all came back to him. Richard had taken him once to a weird, barrow-like hill down on the way to Shuan and the sea. It was a place Richard said he loved; there were tall pines like ships on top of the hillock, and hundreds of these white feathers which must have been pigeons'. Cam could now clearly recall Richard bending down, picking up some of the feathers with a strange, wondering look on his face and saying, quite seriously, 'You know, Cam, I used really to believe that angels came down here once a year, at midsummer, to moult. I always thought they were feathers from angels' wings!'

Now it came back to Cam where the quill pen had come from and he sat there, going over it all in his mind. It had been that year they had gone away for Christmas, far from the coast, to stay with relatives. He remembered how his mother had wanted to visit an ancient library in what seemed to him a weird bit of countryside, low and sunken, as though it might have been under water. There seemed to be hundreds of rooks and jackdaws everywhere, and a smell of bonfires in the air. It was not a place that appealed to him at all; he remembered the car dunting along the single track road, and how he had had the feeling that something strange had happened here. It was no one place in particular; it hung over the whole area, and he was glad that he was not alone. The farm windows were lit like pieces of amber all around, for their visit was in a late afternoon in the winter dark. They came to the library and an old woman came out of her house, unhooked a great iron key and walked with them down the track to the ancient building.

It smelled damp and fusty and bats flitted about in the shadows, and he and Robert played hide and seek. The adults were fascinated by the old books but he knew that he had not liked the place at all; it gave him the creeps, and when at last they left, he looked over his shoulder several times to make sure no one was following them.

Outside, the air was filled with soft feathers of snowflakes, and his uneasiness had vanished in the joy of having snow; maybe they would get stuck, maybe they'd be snowed in and would be unable to get home for the start of school! The old woman was very kind and friendly to them and she asked them in for tea.

The room was bathed in a warm glow; there was a huge open fire giving out a wonderful heat. The woman's husband came in; his gnarled hands looked to Cam as if they were carved out of wood, and he wondered at the thinness of them. They sat and talked while they had tea and hot scones round the fire, and Cam's eyes kept looking out to see if the car was covered yet with snow; he could hardly have borne it if the snow had stopped. The old man then asked if the boys would like to see something special, and he took them over to his desk in the corner and brought out a penknife and two beautiful goose feathers. And he said something Cam could never forget: 'this is the last real penknife'. They watched in fascination as he cut a quick arc of white to make the nib of the quill, and then sharpened its edges with fast, practised strokes. He wrote their names in beautiful flowing letters on a sheet of paper and gave them the quills, one each, and Cam remembered how he had felt this was the most exciting gift he had ever received. His parents too had been impressed. They had left, the good wishes of the old couple following them, as the darkness came in earnest; the snow had changed to a fine mist and the stars shone above like pieces of broken glass. The boys had waved and waved although they could not really see or be seen, until the strange place was just a red glow through the car windows.

Cam turned the quill in his hands and saw that the nib was broken. He felt sad; the old people would no doubt be dead by now; someone else would be looking after the old library. And the man had said his penknife was the last in the world, and Cam had believed him; nobody nowadays made quills out of goose feathers. Somehow he wished with all his heart that he had taken care of the special gift, that he hadn't allowed the nib to get broken. For now he did not know the way back to that place; it was in his mind like a lost Christmas on an old map that had long been discarded.

He looked up and saw that it was raining, but the drops fell through an edge of sunlight that made them look as if they were snowflakes instead. Strange, for the moment it was Christmas that was in his mind; he realised that what he missed was the bigness of childhood Christmases – would there ever be a Christmas like that one again? The bigness of everything seen through a child's eyes; that was gone forever too.

For a moment he felt he wanted to escape from all that was filling his mind from the past; he needed to get it out of his system. Why not go down to Findale with Robert that night, get someone to buy him a drink or two at the Arms? He wanted to be free of his melancholy. What was it that was bothering him anyway? He hadn't been able to shake off his underlying sadness all day. Then he knew it; he must go to see Richard's parents. As soon as he had thought of it, he recognised that he would have to go. It was never easy, but he would do it right away. He drummed down the stairs, still holding the quill in his hand.

The place was always a shock to him. There on the edge of Findale, with the tall oaks round it, a long grey mansion, and a silver car on the driveway in front. He stopped for a moment and looked up at Richard's window, and at once a flood of memories washed over him; he could see Richard's face at the window, could hear his voice calling to him to hurry, that there was something he wanted to show him. How many times had he, Cam, gone along that drive like the wind! There was a giant eel they had trapped and they needed a net; there was a huge ship out at sea and they needed binoculars to see if it was Russian; there was...

He closed the gate and the wind sighed in the fence with a queer whistling sound. Before he was halfway to the door, Barley, the old fat Labrador heard him; he struggled out on to the front steps, barking as though he had heard good news. Then Mrs Brennan came out and joined him, wiping her hands on her apron. Cam's first thought was that she had become much older-looking.

'Oh, good to see you, Cam! Come on in.'

He didn't mind the cultured English of her voice; somehow it was all right, even beautiful. If he'd heard someone in a shop in Findale speaking as she did it might have been different, perhaps, but he had long ago become used to the Brennans' voices. Richard had even begun to acquire quite a Scots edge to his tongue; Cam had taught him phrases, sayings, and had made him repeat them till they sounded acceptable to his ear. They had had many laughs together over their differences in speech. But Mrs Brennan was different, and he accepted her as she was.

'Tom's out just now, I'm afraid,' she said, taking him into the living-room after he had kicked off his boots in the vestibule. 'You have to take us rather as you find us and Saturdays do tend to be somewhat busy.'

'Oh, I'm sorry,' Cam said at once, sitting down and stroking Barley's silky ears.

'Oh no, no, not at all!' she exclaimed, throwing up her hands in horror. 'I'm truly glad to see you, Cam – the place is really lonely when Tom's away. But I'm happy to see you at any time, you know.'

For a second their eyes met, and he saw the shadow that passed across her face, and looked quickly away. His own cheeks burned, but she steadied herself; she did not let the mask break, but instead began to scold Barley for all his moulting and apologised for the state of the carpet.

'Let me get you some tea,' she said. 'Or will you have coffee? All right, just make yourself at home and I'll be back in a moment.'

Now he could allow himself to look at the picture of Richard on the mantelpiece, the smiling face, the hair blond as straw. There was another one of him in his school uniform, beside the big brass clock that kept up its stern beat. Sometimes it was just impossible to believe he was gone; often during the past year he had wakened up, sure that he had heard Richard's running steps on the path outside Ardnish. It seemed like no time at all. He was so far away in his thoughts that she had come in without Cam's noticing, and his eyes were still on the picture; he knew she had seen and was mad at himself.

'Do you know it'll be fifteen months next week?' she said in a brisk voice, pouring the tea and not looking at Cam. And then very quietly: 'D'you still think a lot about him, Cam?'

He nodded as she handed him the cup. He could not speak; he did not dare to say a word. A big black wave seemed to roll at the back of his head, and he strove with all his might to keep himself above it. If he lost control he would never forgive himself. Perhaps she knew; perhaps she saw the strange shining in his eyes as he nodded, and she understood. She must surely have seen it before!

'And you'll be going off to university in the next few days, won't you?' she continued brightly. 'What a change after Ardnish! Aberdeen, isn't it?'

How could she do it, Cam wondered; how could she say all these things so easily? He had been her only son; he'd have been going to university himself at this time, to Aberdeen too perhaps! He didn't want her to go through all this; her mask made it all the worse. But he couldn't say. He didn't know how to tell her to stop pretending, to let down all the elaborate defences she had constructed to keep out the darkness. Why, why had it ever happened? Why had Richard to die? Why were others allowed to have long lives – and Richard had everything to live for? Then he heard himself babbling: 'I'm nervous of going. I've never really been to the city and I'm not even sure what I'm going to study! Seems stupid after all the work for exams and everything, but I suppose I've still plenty of time to decide...

She interrupted him, leaning forward, her face very serious.

'You have to let the people become the grass of the city.'

It was almost as if she hadn't heard a word he had said. 'You were just the same, the two of you – two of a kind. Richard loved everything that ran and sang and leapt. He adored this place from the very first day and he'd have hated to leave it again. I think you'll feel lost at first, Cam; I really do. You may feel it was the maddest thing you ever did, and you'll miss the farm and all the things you love here so badly that it'll hurt. But you must just stick at it. As I said – let people become like the grass you miss. Then in the end you'll be all right.'

5

It was Sunday morning and they were driving down from Ardnish to Findale at a terrible rate of knots. The track between the house and the main road had seen better days, and occasionally Duncan swerved to avoid a particularly deep pothole, causing Robert, in the back, to groan as though in pain. They were on their way to the kirk, and as usual they had left the house with only a few minutes to spare.

'Have you remembered your collection, Cam? Well, where did you leave your jacket last night... Are we ready, then? Well, let's go.'

It was always the same, Cam thought gloomily. It was his mother who saw to it each Sunday that the family went to church. Even Robert, nineteen and broad as a hay bale, seemed to become fairly meek and submissive as she rushed around on a Sunday morning getting them all ready. She sat in the front now, in the passenger seat, checking her hair in the mirror and looking round to see that her sons were reasonably smart. Duncan swerved to avoid a sheep and Robert groaned again. He was in anything but a good mood, Cam realised.

In fact Robert had not had a good night at all. He had gone to the Arms and found a crowd there celebrating Sheila's twenty-first birthday. He wasn't all that keen to stay, but Annie was there and he was desperate to know if there was any chance of winning her back. He had had a drink or two first, but had drunk fast so as to build up his courage, and then he had dared to draw up his chair beside Annie's and begun rather nervously to prattle on about music, and sheep, and second-hand cars...

'Leave me in peace,' Annie said finally, enunciating every word very clearly and coldly. He was taken aback and at a loss to know what to do next, so he returned to the bar after finishing his pint almost in one gulp, and ordered another. Stubbornly he went back to his chair beside Annie, and this time interrupted her talk with Sandy across the table to say: 'I'm going up to Fort William next week. You can come with me if you like.'

'Right, that's it.'

She turned and very calmly poured what was left in her glass into his lap. In a second he was stone cold sober; in a second too everyone there had seen what happened and loud laughter broke out around him. He did not linger for a moment after that. Miserable, humiliated, he went home, feeling he would never show his face in Findale again; far worse, Annie was lost to him for good.

Now he sat in the car wincing at every dip in the road. Worst of all was the fact that he well knew his young brother was gloating; Cam knew fine he had a hangover and was not going to let the occasion pass unnoticed.

'Feeling rough this morning?' he asked sweetly, leaning across to slap Robert on the shoulder. Rob slumped forward and turned venomous eyes on him.

Cam yawned and left his brother in peace. He let his mind wander to the night before, when he had returned from visiting Richard's mother; he had walked by the river, watching the water that splayed down from the falls in wide, white curves. He missed Richard so acutely that it was a physical pain; he wanted to cry out, to vent his sorrow and anger in some way. Again he asked why, why, why had he died? Why did others live to be old, when Richard, so full of life, had been taken so young? There was no justice in it at all! And here he was, next morning, on his way to worship the God who had seen fit to allow this to happen; there seemed to be no sense in it, no sense whatsoever.

The sun came down like a huge net on the glen as the steeple rose out of the trees, and they were there.

'The harvest is past, the summer is ended, and we are not saved. For the hurt of the daughter of my people am I hurt; I am black; astonishment hath taken hold on me. Is there no balm in Gilead; is there no physician there? Why then is not the health of my people recovered?'

The words of the prophet Jeremiah flowed sonorously through the church; the building was filled with grey-blue light, and Cam felt as if the words were a great tide on which he was being carried along...and always, inevitably, carried to the place where Richard had died. For him at that moment, the summer that had ended was Richard; that he had ended was a horrible, inescapable fact. Nothing in the world would bring him back, no doctor, nor all the great spring tides of the Atlantic. In his mind's eye he saw great thick snows coming down over Ardnish and Crossallan and Findale, huge clouds of wet snow on a land that had been drained of all the colours of autumn. He saw himself, as it were, standing at a window looking out at all these deaths – his grandparents', Richard's, even the loss of Rosie was a kind of death to him – and he looked around at the men and women in the pews, many of them quite elderly; one man's hand shook where it lay so thin and old beside his hymnbook. For many of them, the summer had

39

gone. How many of them would be gone before he sat in this pew again? Even his own father was growing old – the eyes were the same as ever, but the face had changed; it was wintering. Soon Robert would have taken his place; the land would pass to him.

Cam felt frightened by all of it. He was suddenly reminded of the phantom horseman whom he had once seen in the larch wood, riding and riding without slowing his pace for a moment. Even as the minister was talking his heart began to speed in a kind of panic; it was like those nights long ago in childhood when his door was shut and the lights were out and he would begin to think of eternity. For ever and ever and ever and ever...fear would grip him and he would want to shut off the thoughts, but could not. Now it all washed over him again; guiltily he realised he hadn't heard a single word of what the minister had been saying.

Then normality returned as his father passed him a sweet; his whiskers tickled Cam's face as he pressed the mint into his palm. Once it had been his grandfather who had done that; now the custom had passed to Duncan. Cam felt almost as though his father had somehow heard his frightened heartbeat and had found a kindly way of wakening him from the panic. What a fool I am; why am I allowing this melancholy to take hold of me just now? He forced himself then to listen to the sermon.

The minister's voice was beautiful – an English accent which somehow had a calming effect upon him at this moment. The Reverend Francis Pearson. Cam remembered the parodies of that name at school assemblies; indeed he recalled the very first time the young minister had stood behind the lectern in the hall, facing two hundred children with hearts like ferrets, ready to pounce, ready to find and pierce the slightest chink in the minister's armour. But they had come away disappointed, able only to pick on his name as a kind of revenge, for he hadn't stuttered once; his voice, then as now, flowed strong and confident, as beautiful as the luminous green water of Avainban Bay.

Richard and he had become curious about the minister. There were all kinds of rumours going round the district about him, mainly because he was unmarried – that he had his eye on this girl or that, or that he had been seen with so-and-so. But the Reverend Frank remained alone in the manse for a few winters, and the gossip began gradually to fade away. Cam's mother maintained that he was a writer as well as a minister and spent much of his time at his books and articles, which was why he had not managed to do half of the visiting his predecessor had, among the elderly and sick. Rumours about him at school tended to be both wilder and nastier; but the one thing that was true was that he was regarded as an outsider and he seemed to have nobody in the community who could be called a close friend.

'Why don't we go to the manse?' Cam suggested to Richard in the attic one evening. It was autumn, with the early dark just beginning.

'Boring,' Richard replied; 'What would be the point?'

'Apples, that's what!' said Cam, taking the catapult from his friend so as to get his full attention. 'Anyway, why don't we spy on him? See what's going on — see if he really is a writer, or what. Come on, Ricky! We could stay at your house. It's Sunday tomorrow...'

For once, Richard had taken quite a lot of persuading, but in the end Cam wore him down and got his Dad to take them into Findale in the car, dropping them off with their bags and boots. It was smirring with rain and almost completely dark by then, but once the red lights of the car had been swallowed they began running up Victoria Road towards the manse.

It was set in a large glebe and almost entirely surrounded with tall sentries of trees and gloomy, high walls. Richard heaved Cam over after him and they both landed with a dull thud on the other side.

'Apple trees over there!' Cam hissed, and they crept through the long grass as the branches of the trees were lashed by the storm above their heads. Cam glanced over his shoulder towards the big house across the lawn and saw a lemon light shining from one room. They sank into the bushes for a long moment to be sure nobody was coming and then prowled on until their eyes made out a tree groaning with fruit; they ran over, and leapt wildly until they managed to catch hold of a bough and ripped off half a dozen huge apples. Cam took a giant bite out of one but in a second his face curdled, and the apple fell from his grasp; he gave a kind of groan of disgust and spat, whispering to Richard: 'Ugh, they're cooking apples!' This rather took the edge off the entire adventure, but they had come this far and certainly didn't feel like turning back.

'Let's go up and see what the minister's doing,' Richard suggested, and they flowed up over the lawn, two black shadows in the vague silvery light of the evening. They reached a gravel path and tiptoed along it, hushing one another urgently when a heel snapped a twig or a step was too loud. Then they came into the lime glow from the open window and shrank down as low as possible, peering now at the man who was seated at his desk, clearly working on the last of his sermon. It was all so ordinary and somehow disappointing. Richard was all for going.

'I'm cold,' he grumbled. 'You promised we'd get back for nine and anyway I dunno what the point is... C'mon, Cam, let's go.'

'Just a second!' hissed Cam, beginning now to feel bolder. 'I'm going to give him a fright, just to see what he does.'

'Cam, you're crazy!' Richard hissed back. 'Anyway, how d'you mean?'

'Throw a pebble, of course.'

Richard was absolutely against the idea; Cam called him a chicken and at the same moment took a pebble and lobbed it so that it banged the glass. Richard lost his nerve and went shooting along the path like a frightened rabbit, while Frank Pearson dropped his pen, began rattling the bolts of the French window and looked outside.

Cam was still crouched on the ground with no idea of what to do next, when the French window opened and golden light spilled out over him as he looked up blindly into the minister's face. 'Cameron,' he said in surprised tones. (He had been up to Ardnish to visit the family and arrange with Morag Mackay about harvest thanksgivings, and knew the boys well enough.) On this occasion Cam was tongue-tied. He could have invented some kind of story but for once his lively imagination deserted him; he simply looked dumbly up at Frank Pearson, his mouth slightly open and his eyes blinking and blinking in the light.

The minister chuckled, relieved.

'Well, I'm glad it's only you,' he said mildly. 'I came out thinking an eagle had crashed into the window! You'd better come in for a mug of cocoa – it's a good time. Are you staying down in the village tonight then?'

Ten minutes later, the Brennans rang up to apologies for their son's inexcusable behaviour and to ask that Cameron Mackay be sent along to the house as soon as possible. Frank Pearson seemed only amused by the situation and came back with cocoa as he had promised; the two of them then sat in front of a rather cheerless gas fire. Although the man was so friendly, Cam had so far managed only to mutter monosyllables.

'Ah, it's a good excuse for me to get away from my desk,' the minister said brightly. 'I never seem to have a minute's peace, you know. I've still got to prepare what I'm going to say to you lot on Monday morning. It's actually going to be a story I made up myself. You see, Cameron, I write books, mostly for children, so I can test you all at school with them – a bit like guinea pigs!'

Cam took a sip of cocoa and looked at the man again. A writer of children's stories! He dropped his guard and couldn't help but feel interest. He began to relax as the minister drew him out; he found himself telling all about his grandfather, and how he had always told them stories when they were small boys.

'Well,' the minister said at last, 'seeing you're so keen on stories you can listen to this one as a punishment! Then I'd better let you go to the Brennans or they'll wonder what on earth has happened to you. Anyway, the story goes something like this:

'There was once a man who lived in a very big city. He had a very fine house of his own and a good job as well. Every day he got up at five past eight and each evening he was home by twenty to six. The most precious thing he possessed was a little silver key. It locked his front door, it opened his office at work, and it unlocked his safe as well. One morning he got up as usual, went out on to the street and searched for the key. But there was nothing! Just the long metal chain to which the key had been attached. The man was bewildered. He looked down drains and he searched under flower pots, he emptied every pocket in a fever of anxiety and he went running up and down as if the moon had fallen from the sky. He would have asked his neighbours for help at that point but he didn't know any of them, and they just peered at him darkly when he tried to look in at their windows. But that was no use anyway because there was no one who had exactly the same key as himself. And it meant he was shut out of his house and his work as well, and he had no idea what in the world he was going to do. So he just wandered through the streets until dark, and then he crept miserably under a bridge and huddled there wrapped in his coat until morning.

'That's about the end of the story really, Cam!' said the minister. 'Not my most cheery one, I'm afraid. But can you perhaps guess something of what I'm trying to say in it?'

43

Cam just looked blank, so he continued: 'Well, it's like this – first, you can't just live for yourself all your life! Life is so much more than simply doing a job and having possessions. It's about finding God; he's the real key. D'you know where I got the idea? Well, it was the first year I was here in the village, and the house and everything else, was still strange to me. I sat here by the fire one night and I must have fallen asleep and dreamed the whole thing. It was one of those dreams you're sure is real because you remember it so clearly.'

It was strange, thought Cam now, how often that odd little story had kept coming back into his mind over the years. In the end, the minister had not used it at assembly after all – maybe he was the only one ever to hear it, or maybe it had been put into a book? But he, Cam, had as it were carried it around like a strange stone he might have found on a beach and could never quite bring himself to chuck back into the water. Sometimes he would think of himself as the man who had lost the key; he saw himself running through the streets of Aberdeen not knowing a soul, and having no idea of how to get home. But he wasn't even sure he had a key to begin with...

The sermon was over and the sunlight had passed through the old church. There was a sound as of many leaves being blown across stone as the congregation turned up the final hymn in their hymnbooks. Robert staggered to his feet – more like an old man than a teenager, Cam thought unkindly – but a moment later, against his will, he felt a slight pang of pity for his brother. After all, Cam had lost Rosie and knew what it felt like, and Robert had been nuts about Annie. Women, he said to himself, are a difficult breed; I think I'd be better off staying clear of them. Staying single would mean a far less troublesome life.

But when Fiona Stewart smiled at him on the way out of church he forgot all of that pretty quickly. He'd never really bothered about her at school because she was so popular; still, a smile like that... Robert had managed to pass the minister without having to shake hands, but then it was Cam's turn.

'All the best for Aberdeen, Cameron!' Frank Pearson smiled as he pumped Cam's hand. 'And see you behave yourself. I've got any number of spies stationed there, you know!'

Cam thanked him warmly, and really meant it. Ever since

44

Richard's death, and that last service which must surely have been one of the hardest ever, he'd believed in the man, even felt real affection for him. He had really seemed to understand how terrible it was for him to lose Richard. Maybe it went back even as far as the night of the apples, Cam thought; he wasn't sure. At any rate he tried to thank him sincerely at this moment; he even stayed longer than he needed to and talked a bit more while Fiona walked away, looking back to see if Cam was coming but then shrugging and giving up on him. He forgot about her almost at once; it didn't matter after all. But it mattered that he talked to this man who had been a good friend to him – the man who was still regarded as an incomer, who was still alone in the big old manse, and still, Cam felt, misunderstood years after he had first come to Findale. It mattered that he didn't go away from here without thanking him.

'I'll get back myself,' Cam said to his mother as he stood with the three of them beside the car. He had made up his mind what he was going to do.

'Och, Cam, you're missing a good dinner!' she lamented.

'Rob can have mine', Cam said nastily, and got a crocodile's grimace from his brother.

Now it was time to be on his own. He wanted to go down to the shore, maybe over to Shuan. The days were going past so quickly; I have to be ready, I have to be at peace with myself. And then aloud:

'I'll not be all that long. It's just that I have something I must do.'

His mother still stood by the car, reluctant to give up.

'Let him go, Morag,' said his father, easing himself into the driving seat. 'But remember, I'm not coming to find you!' he added in mock anger as he started the engine.

Cam stood still until they had gone out of sight, hands in the pockets of his jacket as the wind came at him, tossing the wide branches above his head. The remaining groups were walking away down the sandy track; he could hear their voices and the sudden plumes of laughter although he could make out none of their words. The minister must have gone back into the church again so the place was empty, and Cam was glad. He ran down the shore road through Findale and got on to the path that would take him most directly on to Shuan. With any luck the tide would still be far out and there would be time enough.

Far above his head he heard a buzzard mewing; he stopped at last to search for it, shielding his eyes from the glare of the sunlight. Ah yes, there it was far above, streaming through clouds like a strong branch, circle after circle. It could see the whole of the land – moor, settlement, field, sea, all of them at once. For a second he felt a stab of envy; he could see only one part at a time; he could not put them together. And then he realised how different those he had been thinking so much about were from each other – his grandfather, Rosie, Richard. They were all such different pieces and he did not know how to fit them together. He thought once more of the minister's key; he found himself wishing that he possessed some key that might have solved the puzzle, brought all the broken pieces together to make them one.

He lost sight of the buzzard and turned away, taking the steep path that led to the sea.

6

Far ahead of him, Cam could see the outline of Shuan Island. At low tide it was no island at all; a narrow strip of pearl sand curved out to it from the mainland. But where he stood, the coast was still rocky, indented here and there by tiny cuts of bays, most of it overshadowed by great black buttresses against which the sea came in loud booms. He was looking all the time for Rockdove Cave, a tiny place at the bottom of a deep gully to which there was only one frail, green strip of a path. He knew he had to keep his eyes open for the great quartz boulder, and for the glen on the far side – there it was now! He looked away down and saw the place where Richard and he had gone so often.

I'm wearing all the wrong gear for this, he thought; if I fell here they wouldn't find me for fifty years! The grass was wet and the soles of his shoes smooth – absolutely useless for walking – but he started down all the same, gingerly enough, hanging on to rough rock noses and bits of ledges so as not to rely too much on his feet. Gulls screamed over his head; guillemots and razor-bills went wheeling away to their ledges on the cliffs. Out to sea, in the tiny gap between rock buttresses, Cam saw the long outstretched necks of two cormorants flying low over the water.

Drops of crystal water seemed to be dripping from all the rocks. The noise of the sea was now muffled by a huge rock which sheltered Rockdove Cave, so that he stood in a strange kind of chamber with basalt walls rising sheer on every side, and only a single window of sky above. For a second he panicked, fearing that perhaps his shoes would be too slippery to allow him to climb back to the top again; then he realised he was being foolish, and the ascent was nothing like as hard as it looked.

He began to clamber over the rocks to the narrow strip of beach and the black porthole that was the entrance to the cave. For a second he stopped and just stared at the place, not sure whether he had even been back here since Richard's death. The echoes of our voices must surely be in every rock, he thought; hour after hour, summer after summer they had been here. A vein of sunlight burst through forbidding skies and flooded over the waves so that he turned round, shielding his eyes, suddenly finding his thick wool seater too hot.

All of a sudden he decided to do something mad, something so mad that he would never tell anybody about it. Without any further thought he began tearing off his clothes, throwing them down on the stones at the top of the beach. He had no trunks and no towel, but if he stopped to think he wouldn't do it at all, and he knew all at once that it was simply something he had to do. Straight out into that searingly cold water, his arms hugging his chest, stride after stride until the grey Atlantic was up above his knees; and then he was biting his lips so as not to cry out with the sheer pain of that cold. He glanced in sudden fear around the tops of the promontories, half expecting to see someone watching, imagining for a moment with a brief flicker of amusement what his mother would say if she were there...

'Cam, are you out of your mind? You'll catch your death of cold!'

But he was doing it for his own reasons, which probably neither she nor anyone else would understand; he was doing it in some way to remember Richard. In the end the water was up to his chest and he was breathing fast, feeling the knives of pain that still drove through his thighs and hands. His feet were numb now so that he felt he was staggering on rather as a penguin might have done; the water reached his shoulders and he began to splash about, and then lay on his back and kicked high spray with his feet. He turned and put his whole face under the water, looking about him at the luminous green world, and he scrubbed himself, almost as if he were peeling away a dead skin, an old layer of time, and a past that was gone for ever. Not so as to forget, but that the pain which lingered in his very bones might somehow be healed.

At last he could bear it no longer and he clambered out, slipping on the wet stones and streaming water, shivering in the chill of the wind. He crouched in the entrance of the cave and wished he had had the wit to bring matches, for there was any amount of driftwood for a fire scattered all around on the beach. He dashed about for a while letting the wind dry him, and then, though still damp, struggled into his clothes.

Shivering, he moved deeper into the cave and smelled the musty darkness, the rank smell of pigeons' droppings. He remembered vividly the time Richard and he had thundered down from the ridge above and Richard had blundered into the cave, terrifying a scattering of birds that flapped out from the blackness; today there were no birds, just thick, dark emptiness stretching for some twenty or thirty feet. But he was out of reach of the wind and he settled himself there, sifting memories from the darkness like uncut gems, holding them as it were to the light.

The darkness reminded him of Hallowe'en – an October night that smelled of bonfires, decaying leaves and wet grass. He remembered the sense of excitement there had always been as the great day approached; bonfires were finished off, apples picked, parties arranged.

He began to smile as he remembered the year his parents had had the party up at Ardnish – to smile, but at the same time to cringe. Richard had been there, of course; it was a couple of years after the Brennans had come to live in Findale. A good number of his parents' friends had been there, and it was the time that Rob had just started going out with Annie, so her parents were there to meet the Mackays for the first time.

The bonfire had been lit down at the bottom of the lower field and a mighty stack it had been too, since his father had had to cut down a rotten old tree and great chunks of it were piled among the branches. There was hot punch in the kitchen for the grown-ups, and hot orange and toffee apples for the children; Cam remembered how the two of them had run about here and there, shouting and laughing, nearly out of their minds with excitement.

He recalled running up to the larch wood just to get a good view of everything. The fire had been lit by his father and was a tiny orange ball in the gathering darkness; up above, the stars were sparkling like fires themselves. Maybe that's what they were, Cam used to think, great fires beside which giants crouched in the skies, watching the earth. On a night like that, dark things might happen, magic and secret things, beyond explanation. He shivered and looked at the grey shadow of the rocks up in the top field and wondered again how they had come there. The world was not explained; the teachers at school had not explained it. To him it was strange and wonderful, filled with the most intriguing secrets.

All of this was before the guests had begun to arrive. The hours had gone by like tortoises, but at long last people started to come. He left his outpost and went down to the house; the first sparklers splintered silver in the hands of children; a group had gathered beside the bonfire, talking and laughing. A number of older children from Findale trooped up to Ardnish, all dressed in weird outfits and with swinging turnip lanterns; they sang two verses of a song, forgot the rest, and were rewarded with nuts, apples and cake. Then Richard arrived.

'You have to see the den – I finished it today!' Cam had shouted excitedly, dragging Richard away at high speed up to the larch wood. They reached the trees and then crouched to enter a low tunnel, all covered with branches which Cam had taken from the tree his father had felled; this led through to a domed cell hidden at the back of one of the larches. He was as proud as if he had personally built St Paul's Cathedral. Richard had been suitably impressed, but was cold.

'Listen!' Cam said then, getting up suddenly in excitement from where he was crouching, 'Why don't we sneak back and get a bottle of wine from the cellar? That would warm us up all right. My Mum's been using it for making the punch. We could come back here and make a fire – it'll be hours yet till the fireworks start!'

Richard had not been too sure. 'They'll kill us if they find out!' he said.

But Cam was up and on his way. 'There'll never be a chance like this again,' he shouted as he ran down the hill. 'Come on, it's a brilliant idea!'

They got down to the cellar and Cam grabbed a bottle. Who should they meet just as they were coming out of the basement door but Robert, involved in a long kiss with Annie. For once he was not interested in Cam, and the two boys slunk away to the wood and dived gratefully into the den. They set about making a fire, using nearly a boxful of matches before it was lit. Then they poured themselves a couple of glassfuls, clinked them in mid-air, and drank.

'Don't notice any effect,' said Richard in disappointed tones after a few minutes, taking another slug in case he had missed something. Cam remembered trying to sound professional.

'Hm, not bad,' he had pronounced after a critical sip. 'Pour me some more; this is good stuff,' he added later. The bottle seemed to last an unbelievably short time.

All of a sudden they heard a terrific bang and the two of them jumped like startled rabbits as a shower of red and purple sprayed the sky.

'Help, the fireworks!' Richard breathed in horror; Cam started to his feet, but the ground came up to meet him and he fell in a heap. The two of them began to giggle uncontrollably; then Richard got to his feet more cautiously and very gingerly the two of them started down the hill, trying hard not to stagger. The harder they tried, the worse they got.

The whole crowd was arranged in a semi-circle on one side of the bonfire whilst out in the stubble crouched Duncan Mackay, setting up a line of fireworks. Head after head turned as the two zombies tripped and staggered their way towards the fire. Rob stepped out from the rest, holding Annie's hand, leaning forward to make sure it really was his brother. Then, 'You're drunk!' he said in a loud voice; every head turned, and suddenly somebody gave a loud chuckle, and the whole lot of them started to laugh. His father didn't bother to light the next firework; he turned round to see what was going on and saw the two swaying Hallowe'en ghosts.

Cam laughed to himself now as he crouched in Rockdove Cave. He recalled the many lectures the two of them had been given on the dangers of alcohol, and how Richard had been banned from

Ardnish for long enough afterwards. They were never allowed to forget the episode, he thought ruefully; whenever people talked about Hallowe'en or bonfires, you could be sure this was the first thing they'd mention. And he and Richard were never allowed anywhere near the cellar again.

'Och, we were good for them!' he found himself wanting to say aloud to an invisible Richard before the familiar stab, the awful sinking feeling, came once more. How was it that he could still forget, still imagine they were doing something together? It was bad enough in dreams, when his presence would be so vivid... Then he shook himself mentally. Why am I tormenting myself, going over all this? What does it matter – these are only childish pranks which mean nothing to anyone else? Why don't I just go, get on with the next part of my life, be at peace within myself? And then he seemed to answer his own question: it does matter. Richard was wound tightly round the first part of my life; I can't just go away as if he'd never existed.

And then, all of a sudden, a darkness fell upon him and he felt desperate to get away from the place; it was almost as though Richard's dead body had been carried on the water into the little cove. The shadow of death fell like a folded kestrel, and Cam felt fear, real fear as he began to scramble up and away, back over the slippery stones, up and up until he had climbed the steep face safely and was standing breathless on the ridge, shuddering as he stared back down into the cove. Had it been his own imagination? If only he hadn't been born with such a vivid one, as his father so often told him! Or had something really come at that moment, something dark and terrible?

He shivered and broke away over the headland, letting the wind that drove up bitter cold from the sea blow away the blackness of his spirit. He knew he was going to have to hurry if he was going to reach Shuan before the tide changed and the sands were cut off from the mainland. It would take him a good half-hour to get up that far and he was going quickly, pounding along the jagged ridge that extended along the length of the coast, wishing he had something more suitable on his feet than his best shoes. He was suddenly very hungry and thought longingly of the good Sunday roast his mother would have served by now; he searched his pockets but found nothing – not even a scrap of chocolate.

It was as he came over another bit of ground and turned inland

51

for a moment that he caught sight of the dragonfly. He stood stock still, forgetting his hurry, wide-eyed with amazement. Often enough he had seen dragonflies around hill lochs in the middle of summer, looking for all the world like tiny helicopters, nudging the reeds and droning low over the surface of the water. But never before had he seen one so close, landed motionless on a clump of dead heather. Carefully Cam leaned forward, making hardly a sound as he tried not to breathe at that moment; every second he expected the beautiful creature to fly away, but to his surprise it remained, until he was right over it and had his hand out, trembling, to allow it to clamber aboard. It was like the bar of a brooch, a tropical blue, kingfisher blue even; as it moved up on to his finger he saw that the four wings were made out of hundreds of tiny panes, all of them shining like the paper of Chinese lanterns.

What a tale he could have invented, if Richard had been here! They used to bounce ideas off one another, sometimes making up new games, sometimes telling a story, hungry at the end for encouragement or praise, awarding marks on a carefully constructed scale. Cam sat down gently on the heather; the dragonfly still clung to his hand.

'I will make up a story!' he said aloud. 'It'll be about you, and I'll try to think of some of the things I know Richard would have thought of.' He let his mind wander, spinning out ideas in a hundred directions, like a spider's web, to trap mad thoughts.

'All right. There was once a young boy who was kept prisoner by Fan, the horrible king of the underworld.' Richard had invented Fan; there was even a cave near Avainban Bay which had been identified as the entrance to Fan's lair. 'He was miserable the whole time; he missed the sun, he missed the colours of flowers and leaves and ferns and seashells. One day he felt he couldn't bear it any longer. He went and begged Fan on his knees to let him out for just one day so that he could see the spring again. Amazingly, Fan finally agreed. The boy ran as fast as he could, up and up through all the tunnels and chambers of the underworld, until at last he came up into the early morning sunshine. The sun was just coming up over the sea and everywhere he looked, green things were beginning to grow after the long hard winter.

'The wee boy went running around like mad, running and laughing in the sunshine, determined to see as much of the beauty of spring as he possibly could. He went on drinking it all in and the day passed far too quickly; suddenly he realised the sun was starting to go dark in the sky and it wouldn't be long before the night came. He knew with a sinking heart that he had to go back to Fan's horrible kingdom but he wanted to take something with him, just one special thing, so that he would never forget that wonderful day. Away over in the west where the sun was about to set there was the most beautiful bit of blue sky and the boy stretched up on his tiptoes, took enough to fill his hand, and put it safe in his pocket. Then he ran the whole way back down into Fan's prison.

'He thought and thought about what he should make. And in the end, he took the piece of sky and smoothed it in his hands until it was long and thin. Then he got a bit of shiny metal from the cave where he was kept and he hammered it out until it was thinner and lighter than a feather. He shaped all the wee bits for hours and hours until he was quite satisfied with them and then, very, very carefully, he put them on to the piece of sky and fitted them exactly. Then he held what he had made gently in his hands and blew softly. Sure enough the creature took off into the air and went humming round his head. The boy was absolutely thrilled; he jumped and sang for sheer happiness.

'But then Fan came in to see what the noise was all about and he shrieked in terror; he couldn't stand anything made of light. He covered his eyes and began to make strange whimpering noises whenever the bright creature came near him; it began to fly round and round his head, and gradually Fan just crumpled into a ball, and he seemed to melt away. And in the end there was nothing left of him at all.

'The boy could hardly contain his joy; he called to the creature and it came and landed on his hand. He wanted then to give it a name, but he found he had forgotten what things in the real world were called, and the only thing he could think of was that there were huge fiery beasts at the centre of the earth which kept the ovens of Fan's kingdom alight. So he decided he would call the little creature a dragonfly, and he carried it all the way up to the top of the world before setting it free.'

Cam found himself unconsciously looking over at the next tussock, almost believing Richard was sitting there listening to every word, eyes narrowed in judgement; Cam imagined him rocking gently back and forth as he had done a hundred times, the smallest edge of a smile on his lips as he grudgingly nodded: 'Not

53

bad, not bad.'

The dragonfly suddenly lifted off from Cam's hand and thrummed away through the air till it was lost to view. He found himself wondering whether it had really been there; it was as if he might have imagined the whole thing.

Now he realised how much time he had wasted; he must get down to the beach at Shuan and across to the island without any more delay. He would be mad at himself if he had missed the tide now; he had only a few days left and most of his stuff was still waiting to be packed. All his time was precious.

Cam remembered how Fleet used to cover this ground with the two of them – for all the world, he thought, like a black and white waterfall as she flowed through the heather effortlessly ahead of them. He recalled clearly the only time they had lost her; it was when she had decided to go off and roll in a dead sheep on one of the ledges high above Avainban. What a stink there had been! Richard and he could hardly bear it; they had had to carry her to the first rock pool they could find and dump her in it to get rid of the worst of it. Even after that, though, she wasn't exactly popular when they took her home.

As Cam looked across the last headland he could clearly see the long white spar of land that curled out to Shuan. There was maybe an hour or so left before the waves came over the narrow peninsula and covered it again. Nobody now lived on the island; all that remained of the only house was a grey hump of rubble and an area of grass that might once have been a field. Richard and he used to declare that they would build a cottage there one day; when their talk grew wild and bold they would dream of all kinds of things – they'd have a boat to explore the coast; a diving bell to find the wreck of the Spanish galleon; a summer house of their very own on Shuan. They knew every inch of the island; they had made maps of it over and over again; they would put in all the place names they invented from each new visit. In Cam's eyes, Richard's names were always better than his; he recalled how he had often felt he stood in his friend's shadow and had, in a sense, needed to fight to be an equal. But then it was also true that he, Cam, had been the bolder and stronger of the two. There was nothing he wouldn't jump off, or be the first to creep in and explore.

He came down to the shore and five oystercatchers took off,

screeching at him in panic. Away in the north he could see the dim
outline of the hills of Rum and Eigg; fantasy peaks they were,
when the clouds were thick and grim as that one on the horizon.
His nerve nearly failed him now, but as he looked across the strip
of sand towards Shuan he saw the shadow of a boy with straw-
blond hair, calling and waving to him, bringing him across.

'Come on, Cam! The tide's nearly turning, and there's starfish
and flounders everywhere...'

7

Cam started across over the ribbed patterns of the sand, and then
bent down and took off his shoes and socks so that he could splash
through the pale water. The whole of his view was taken up by
Shuan now – the red-gold rocks that ringed its outer limits and the
main dome of darker stone that made up the centre. Around that
hill, in little glens and coves, were buried stories. They were like
fossils, different ages, the memories of long summers. He wanted
so desperately now to reach the place that his heart began
hammering in his chest. Once he had been round the island in a
boat, but that was all; when Richard died, a book had, as it were,
been closed, a book that he could hardly bear to read again. He had
never come back. Yet here he was again; now it seemed to him
that he longed for this special place with all his heart, and that it
did not matter what happened, just as long as he got across to
Shuan again.

Looking all around, it seemed that there were signs of storm
everywhere; yet, in the very eye of it, brightness burst upon the
water so clear and white that it almost hurt his eyes as it was
reflected. The wind rushed over the shallow pools at the edges of
the sand-strip, ruffling them and changing their colours, yet Cam
felt no cold at all. He kept to the sandy pathway, hardly making a
sound as (from time to time) he drove his feet through the grey
pools. There were sudden booms of sand as flounders, almost the
very colour of the sand, swept out into the safety of the deeper
water. There were shoals of minute sand-eels too, colourless mini-

snakes swaying together in their hundreds, thousands, turning like perfectly trained soldiers to surge away into a new place. He marched for a time in step with a green crab as it thudded its way out to Shuan. Around him and above him, countless white birds screeched continuously – gulls, terns and shearwaters. Further out at the northern end of the island he saw other birds rising into the air and crashing straight down like white bombers; as they hit the sea, great plumes of spray rose up, tall geysers of water. He smiled to himself as he realised there must be a good shoal of fish off the island to attract such a multitude of gannets.

In the end he got over to the island. The strip of sand now curled round wide to the left, making a long arch of beach on which there were tidemarks of miniature shells – scallops, periwinkles and cowries. But Cam did not stop there, much as he loved to pick up tiny, perfect specimens, particularly of cowries, his favourites; instead he walked on and up among the huge boulders of rock that were like giants' dice, stones that had obviously once rolled down from the slopes of Cruachan, the highest hill on Shuan. In among those rocks, he recalled, that's where we found the treasure!

He couldn't remember now whether it had been early spring or late autumn. At any rate, he knew it had been a fierce day, with the wind hurling about their heads and the rain seeming to come from every direction into their faces. Richard and he had decided to go over to the island because of the high seas there had been in the last few days. Now and again they would find the oddest things washed up on the beaches – a broomstick, a globe, even a coconut. And they were determined to go to Smugglers' Cave.

'Now be careful you two, when you're going over to Shuan,' Duncan Mackay warned them as he laboured with the bales of hay. 'The waves are as high as a horse; it's a wicked day.'

The two of them made their way down to the beach and across like the wind, but as they rushed up among the great shining black boulders Richard, who was ahead of Cam, stopped and pointed down to the edge of the sand.

'Tea bags!' he said then in disgust. 'A whole load of them must've been washed up – look.' He clambered back down, hands deep in the pockets of his anorak as it was so cold and wet. It was hardly worth looking through really, just a burst-open sack it seemed, containing nothing more valuable than tea. Cam was kicking over the sodden heap when all of a sudden he turned something up and jabbed at it like a gannet.

'Ricky!' he shouted, squatting down among the mess of bags. Richard came over at once, his eyes searching through the driving rain to see what Cam was holding. It was a tiny cotton bag, for all the world like just another tea bag, only whiter. Around the four sides it had been precisely sewn up. And inside there were tiny stones.

Cam allowed his friend to hold the bag, passing it over with hands that trembled.

'Maybe it's diamonds,' he breathed as he turned his wet face up to Richard.

'Maybe it's drugs,' Richard said as he examined the minute package. He was unbelievably jealous, that it had been Cam who found the treasure. And then: 'Let's open it and see.'

'No!' Cam nearly ripped the precious cotton bag from his grasp. 'No! I want to wait till we get home!'

They went round to the cave after that, but their hearts weren't in it any longer. Cam kept turning the bag in his hands and wondering, wondering all the time. They were stones all right, but what kind of stones? It was almost more exciting not knowing, just hearing them patter over one another as he tipped the bag back and forward between his fingers. It was like a strange pillow, this tiny bag that had floated over the waves.

'Tea comes from Sri Lanka,' Richard mused as they sat later, hunched inside the cave, while the rain continued to come down in sheets outside. 'There are lots of gemstones there, my dad says – sapphires and topazes, emeralds too. Maybe they were a gift to somebody, the person who was getting the tea? Maybe they were a kind of secret sign that something was going to happen, a deal between mafia agents...'

Cam let Richard go on using his ever-fertile imagination; at the moment he didn't really care all that much about the story; one day it would perhaps become more important than the stones, but not yet, not yet. All he wanted to know was what they were, for this was his treasure, the first real treasure he had ever found.

'Let's go home,' he said suddenly and stood up to go.

Even now the early darkness was beginning and as they crossed the spit of sand, the world seemed grey and dead around them. They plodded along like a couple of hedgehogs, withdrawn into their anoraks as they splashed back the long miles to Ardnish. But Cam was far away in his own inner kingdom; a proud drum beat in his heart. Tight under white knuckles he clutched the precious cotton bag.

Now, years later, he looked down once more at the place where he had found it. There was nothing left of the consignment of tea, nor of the sack which had contained it. He couldn't avoid the thought that came to him – Richard was gone as well. And he would have given all the treasure in the world to bring him back.

The stones had turned out to be opals. Tiny things they were, and milky, but with a strange reddish hue in the heart of each. What mattered to him was that he had found them; they were treasure.

Cam started up now from the beach, and soon reached the bottom of the hill. The path was scarcely visible among the great mauve clumps of heather, but he did not hesitate and climbed quickly; after about a hundred feet he was warm, and his breath was coming quickly; as he rose on to the shoulder of Cruachan the breeze began to cool his face and hands. An occasional startled grouse exploded near him out of the heather. On and on he climbed until at last he stood panting on the summit. The sunlight fell in an orange-gold path over the sea; he looked away out as far as his eyes could reach, and there was nothing, no sign of a ship, no land. Nothing between here and New York, and it felt awesome, terrible, huge and wonderful all at the same time. Then he looked down to the western shores of Shuan and to the tiny secret beach of Camas and his eyes began to burn with unshed tears; and, despite himself, the tears came and he rubbed them away angrily, even although there was nobody to see him.

Last June it had happened, at the very height of the summer. The days were so long that they seemed to run into one another; the nights were blue and filled with the sound of the curlews and the breathing of the sea. The holidays had just begun, and he and Richard had planned out each day months before; it seemed as if they had been wishing and dreaming ever since Christmas. That particular day was no different; Ardnish looked and sounded just the same; all the windows of the house were open and there was sand on the kitchen floor.

At six in the morning a stone cracked against Cam's bedroom

window. He had had a bad dream, though he couldn't now recall what it had been about, and his head was heavy after too many long, sun-filled days. And it was Saturday. After a few moments he stumbled out of bed, still more than half asleep, and swam through the blue shadows of his room to open the curtains; a blast of steely light caught his eyes. He shoved the window open and, half-blind, peered down at Richard.

'I'm going over to Shuan, to Camas! It's perfect for swimming, Cam!'

Cam groaned. 'Not yet!' He ran his hands through his hair. 'It's early and I want to sleep!'

'Lazy old sheep!' Richard taunted. 'C'mon,' he begged. 'It'll be brilliant; once you're up you'll not feel tired. You promised, Cam, remember!'

'I'll be over later,' Cam said finally and started lowering the window; he crept back to bed, already feeling a bit guilty; he had said yesterday that he wanted to go over to Shuan early in the morning to swim. It took him longer than usual to get back to sleep; Robert was crashing about in the next room and then holding a loud conversation with his father. Then at last the place went back to silence and he slept without dreaming, dead to the world.

In no time, it seemed, his mother was shaking him and calling his name, and at first he thought he was dreaming.

'Come downstairs,' she was saying. 'Come down right away!' And he heard her crying; he could hardly remember such a time, except for once when Rob had been brought home by the police...

His head seemed to be full of cotton wool and he staggered about trying to find his clothes; he saw it was after twelve and could hardly believe it. He got on a shirt and trousers, and raced down the stairs; ever after, he could remember how his stomach had been churning with fear, and the awful taste in his mouth. Always, at the thought of that terrible morning, the sickness returned, and the memory of stark fear. In the kitchen were his mother and father; they were hunched over the table, their arms folded as though their stomachs hurt. The room was filled with blue light and birdsong and warmth, but in the atmosphere was something of doom.

'What is it, what's wrong?' he asked, thinking first that he had done something dreadfully wrong. But they told him that Richard

59

was dead.

Attie Duncan, a fisherman from a house near Findale, had been out that morning laying creels off Shuan, when he had seen something bumping the rocks beside Camas beach, and found the body. It had been about ten in the morning.

After that everything was confusion, a kind of haze in Cam's mind. He remembered how he had just gone on staring and blinking, saying nothing, feeling as though the room was swaying about him. He did not break down. His parents held him; even Rob's hand was there, but they were all distant; he seemed to see and hear them through blue water. It was like having a fever; it reminded him of times when he had been ill as a child and the pillow would seem to bury him and the ceiling was huge and far away. It was as if he had been wrapped in cotton wool and he did not know how to get away from it.

After that, the days seemed to run into each other like the carriages of a crashed train. He did not go out; he was stranded in his own small world, as if he too had drowned and would never come back to life again. But five days afterwards, he went downstairs when everyone else was out, and there, sitting on the table, was a photograph of Richard and himself, taken by Mr Brennan the previous winter. When he saw it his eyes welled with tears; a stone wall cracked within him and he realised, he understood, he knew what had happened. He cried as though his heart would break, until he was too tired to cry any more. And guilt ate at him; he had failed to go with Richard as he had promised, and the awful thought came to him that perhaps, if he had gone, it would never have happened at all. When he had stopped crying he went outside, trembling and weak as an invalid, but he could not get away from the awful truth; the face of Richard was in everything he saw.

Fifteen months had gone by and now he looked down on Camas. Never again would he swim at that place which had been specially theirs; it just was not possible.

Nobody ever really understood why Richard had drowned. A blue, still morning with almost no wind, but little ridges of waves coming in to the shore, gentle and luminous. Perhaps, they thought, he had tried to swim out to the cluster of rocks away over to the west of Camas, and had been taken by a sudden cramp. Perhaps he had lost his footing when clambering over the outer rocky shore, and had fallen and injured his skull, for there had been a wound to his head, a deep cut at the base of his neck.

In the weeks and months that followed, speculation went on and on; there were new articles in the local paper following the inquest; there was always talk in Findale. Sometimes a well of anger would rise in Cam; none of this mattered, for nothing would bring Richard back from death. The Brennans shut themselves up in their own world, and did not come out until the reporters had grown tired of the case and had found a new story to dismember. Only when the winter came at last, and with it the snow, did it seem to Cam that something was washed away; the first colours came back with the spring.

It shocked Cam after that how quickly he began to forget. He would be in the middle of doing something, carried away, when all of a sudden his face would be slapped by guilt. He felt it was a kind of betrayal. In time, though, even that passed; it was simply a fact that his world was changing, and it was no longer one that had known Richard. New experiences came; soon he would be sitting his last exams, soon he would be away at university. In a way, Richard was now younger than himself. He was growing away from him and could no longer be part of the same world.

Nonetheless, Cam felt Richard's presence strongly on such a day. Here, in this landscape they were equals, and so it would always be. This place they had shared completely, and if Cam felt him to be anywhere it was surely here – in the clear water, in the caves, on the moors. Sometimes he did not know which was worse – to forget, or to remember: both had their cost, both hurt. He had not come back to Shuan since that day in early summer last year; until now he could not face it. Even now he was not sure whether he had the strength to remain. While he had been climbing he had promised himself he would go down to Camas and the cave, but now he did not feel he could, not yet. He despised himself for his weakness, but it was no good; in the end he turned away and began the fast descent to the shore as the tide was turning, and only an hour remained until the sea would cover the path again.

He thought of the weird dreams which had begun to plague him in the weeks after Richard's death; as he remembered, cold fingers of fear descended his back. The minister had visited Ardnish several times to talk to him; he had listened with understanding to

Cam's fears, had heard of the deep guilt he felt through having failed to go with Richard on that morning. Although it helped to talk of the sickness that was deep in his spirit, his head was still full of thoughts and imaginings, and for a long time the dreams still came.

For some reason they were not of Camas itself, but rather of the other side, the gap between Shuan and the mainland. Always the land on both shores was very high and forbidding, like the shoulders of giants. It always seemed to be twilight, unclear and full of dark shadows. Each time he, Cam, appeared to be waiting right at the edge of the shore as a strange boat carved its way through the water towards him. It was a large craft, with a metal gangway descending into the water as the boat drew closer. There on the deck stood a single figure, a man with his legs planted wide and his hands on his hips. He looked straight at Cam and his eyes shone white, like strange dead moons in a night sky.

In this recurrent dream, Cam would always wake up before the boat came to land. All the same the dream scared him; on one occasion, he remembered, he was strongly tempted to go through the house to his parents, but he didn't go, terrified that Robert might find out or his father and mother think him silly. He was not as close to them as he had once been; he felt he did not know them so well. But in the end the dreams passed and did not return. And Frank Pearson came for a last time to Ardnish to talk to him.

He wondered how it would be in the future. The sand between Shuan and Avainban was growing less and less as he walked across, and no doubt it would be just the same with all the things he remembered; bit by bit they would be covered. The time would come when he would struggle to think of Richard's face, or to remember the way he laughed; the thousands of words, the stories they had shared, would fail and become only the bones of things, nothing more than names. But still there was a sense in which Richard would be with him for ever! Somewhere deep inside him a certain special feeling was aroused when his name was mentioned, an inexplicable sensation that would not, he felt, ever die or diminish but which was always there, strong as the scent of bog myrtle over a moorland, quick as the taste of salt from a high-kicked wave of the sea.

Soon, dark would come. As Cam reached the top of the ridge on the far side, he caught sight of the bar of light – like a bar brooch shining gold – that was Findale. It was a long walk yet, but he did not mind. In a way he did not really want it to end at all, not, at least, until all the tangled threads had been brought together in his mind, and he felt he had made some kind of sense of them.

The darkness fell as a weight across his shoulders. Time frightened him these days; he was conscious as never before of its passing, of so many journeys and changes, of his own powerlessness; he had reached a landmark, the end of the first part of his life. A whole new era lay ahead. As he walked back to Ardnish with the rain now falling spearlike against his face, he felt in a strange way that Richard was somehow to be envied. It had only been in the last year, the year since he died, that Cam had felt older, more threatened, almost as if a load had been placed on his back. The load comprised many things to do with responsibility; before, he had never given a second thought to danger, the passing of time, or the possibility of death. It was as if he knew their names, but they were far too remote to be of any consequence to him. Then, before the end of that summer, Richard had died, and his perspective had suddenly had to change; now he could no longer run away from reality. Once again the enormity of it all struck Cam. Richard had gone out barefoot and carefree in the wild beauty of that summer morning, and had run without thinking, without fear of danger, into the sea. But in a strange and terrible way, Cam felt, he had perhaps died in time, he had died before it was too late.

He stood stock still as this thought, which he scarcely understood himself, came to him; he was on the edge of a sharp ridge, looking down on the white anger of the sea as it rose in storm; he could look inland from here too, out over the rough pasture land towards Ardnish, with all its memories of his grandfather. Maybe these thoughts were mad; maybe they were his own way of accepting Richard's death without becoming twisted and bitter in the face of such terrible loss. He did not know. He was tired of trying to make sense of it all, tired of trying to square so many circles...

All at once, the strange story the minister had told him all those years ago, about the man who lost his key, came into his head. Frank Pearson had said that God was the real key, that everything else fell into place when he was at the centre of one's life. Maybe he was right; he would have to think more about it. But not now;

the emotions of the day had exhausted him. The weather was worsening all the time. As he steered his way home through driving rain and wind in the gathering darkness, he felt for all the world like a battered ship heading for port, knocked off course from time to time by sudden big waves.

He would not think any more, he decided. His father had always told him he took life far too seriously; he was aware that this was true, but neither knew how to change, nor really wanted to. But perhaps he should try to do what his father said – let time shed the old skin and make him a new one.

At last he swam into the warmth of the lights and shivered gratefully as he thudded the mud from his boots. He opened the back door and stepped inside. There was no one in the kitchen; he walked across and opened the far door; from the other end of the house there came the sound of singing and a fiddle. Wet through as he was, he slushed through the house in his soaking clothes and opened the door of the sitting-room. Half a dozen faces lit up with smiles.

'Welcome home at last, Cam!' It was his good friend Danny, the postman. 'We just decided on the spur of the moment to come and give you a bit of a ceilidh, boy, to send you on your way!'

The tiredness seemed to leave him in an instant; the warmth of the fire reached him, and burned his freezing cheeks.

'Great!' he said. 'Just give me a few minutes to change and I'll be with you!'

He was glad; he was really glad. They would never know how much it meant to him.

8

The music went on until three in the morning; it seemed to go on to a timeless place where all that mattered were the songs themselves, and the singing. When the last of his friends had gone Cam went outside to still his racing thoughts. The stars were glittering like cut gemstones on the dark back-cloth of the sky; there was no moon now, but the skies were intensely bright. He stood there in silence for a long time; he didn't even have a sweater on, but just went on standing there by the back door, getting his breath back, getting his balance back, feeling almost as if it was music and not blood that coursed in his veins. Into the songs he had poured all his despair over Richard; the best songs were the sad ones, he always felt. But at the same time he was aware of having also poured into them the celebration, the thanksgiving. In the end he began to realise that he had ceased striving to make sense of it all; deep inside of him there were at last the beginnings of peace.

'Are you going to bed now?'

He turned abruptly round and saw Robert standing there in the kitchen, a black expression on his face. He had left the ceilidh hours before.

'Some of us have to work tomorrow, you know,' he added sourly.

Already he had turned away and Cam couldn't think of an answer. It had always been the same, ever since he was a child; when anyone came out with some accusation, no matter whether it was true or utterly false, he could never manage to think in time. The words would haunt him for ages afterwards and by then he would have a hundred answers flying like bees around his head; but it was too late, it was always too late.

'You'll be glad to know they're all gone now,' he wanted to hurl the words indignantly at Rob's back, but his brother was already disappearing up the stairs and Cam had no wish to waken his parents. He sighed, went inside and shut the door quietly; the joy of the night had been smashed by Rob. There had been no need for him to speak like that! Had he not seen Cam's friends leave? But of course he'd only done it to annoy; he'd timed it perfectly so that Cam had no chance to answer. Now his heart banged within him, frustrated and enraged. Always, always it had been like this; always he had been the loser. At that moment he felt he really hated his brother – not for his action just now, but for all the past years of things, the triumphant words and expressions, the winning of countless arguments, time after time. He had always been not simply the younger brother but the weaker brother.

He could not go to bed yet; tired though he was, there was no point – he would never sleep. He went back into the sitting-room and put another couple of logs on the fire; better here in comfort than lying awake with all the worms of past memories writhing in his head! The thing was that he didn't really want revenge on Rob; after all, the two of them were grown-up now – Rob was nineteen. Maybe he felt worse about it now because of his memories of Richard; maybe he was frightened because he now realised things could happen so fast, without the slightest indication. Death sent no warning. Richard had been taken away in a split moment, and for ages afterwards Cam had blamed himself bitterly for having let him go alone to Shuan. He had suffered remorse over the death of his best friend; how much more would he suffer if anything should happen to the brother who was his enemy?

In a way he knew it was crazy to think of the possibility of death like this. The chances were that Rob would still be stomping around Ardnish in his eighties! But the thing was, nobody could be sure. Cam knew that once he had trusted life, had trusted it blindly, taken everything for granted. It was true of course that his grandfather had died, so he had known death; unconsciously, though, he had linked it with the old. Then Richard had died, and suddenly all that was turned upside down. Nothing was safe.

Now he began to think how much he wanted to heal this rift with his brother before he left, for his own peace of mind as much as anything. All he asked for was an end to the war, nothing more. But he did not see how to accomplish this; there seemed to be no way. He looked round towards the window and his attention was caught by a flutter of something white against the pane. Must be a moth, he thought. He got up and went over, to see that out of the darkness tiny flakes of snow were drifting down. It was almost beyond belief – this early in autumn! Mind you, the seasons had been so weird of late that it wasn't perhaps all that strange, and it had certainly been cold enough earlier. Probably by the morning it would be gone and forgotten.

It brought something to mind, though, and he smiled. Ages ago the whole family had been to some ceilidh or other – maybe it was the year they had gone to the ancient library and had been given the quill pens? He wasn't sure. At any rate there had been plenty of snow about and they had had the most awful job to get the car down the farm track to the place. What he recalled vividly, though, was the quality of the snow – it was that wonderful kind which came so seldom, flakes like feathers from the wings of snowy owls, huge and fluffy, perfect for sliding and snowballs. He remembered how madly excited he had been, asking if they were likely to be snowed in, while his poor father kept scraping the snow from the windscreen as well as having to get out and clear the middle rut of the track so that the car's undercarriage would survive.

At last they had arrived and Cam remembered it as a big building built around a central courtyard. The lights from the low windows were a beautiful orange-red colour and they made him shiver with anticipation. Inside there were maybe a dozen or so folk in a room that appeared to be on several levels. He was the youngest there, and was allowed to sit on the floor right in front of the fire, so that his cheeks burned with the heat. Then began an evening of songs and stories and talk; he became more and more uncomfortable there on the floor, not sure whether it was better to cross his legs or to kneel or sit with his back to a chair. He kept trying to catch his father's eye to tell him it was time to go, but Duncan was far too carried away with the night's entertainment, and eventually Cam gave up in despair.

Then he simply had to go to the loo, so he made his way out at the end of a song, balancing carefully between feet and instruments till he had reached the door and then found his way upstairs. As he returned to the room he stopped and looked out of the window to monitor the snowfall. The wind had died away to almost nothing and the flakes by this time were very thin, as fine as threads. Darkness had fallen and a great silver back of moon was rising from among the trees. It was then Cam had the most wonderful idea; he leapt to the front door, hauled it open and brought in two mighty handfuls of snow. With a tremendous sense of triumph he put one into each of Rob's boots, just before their hostess came out of the room to guide him back for the final songs of the evening.

By now it was fairly late; Duncan Mackay, carried away as he was in enjoyment of the entertainment, remembered the clock at last. Cam could scarcely keep a smile of triumph from his face as the family moved towards the door and he had to be sharply reminded by his mother to say thanks for the evening. He was careful to be first out as Rob roared in agony and rage at the discovery of the snow. He hopped about the yard, hurling bits of snow at his brother, but unable to walk properly because of the sheer discomfort of his feet. Cam was unable to contain his joy; it was all he could do to keep a few steps away from his enraged brother; he was out of breath with laughter. For weeks afterwards Rob would hardly speak to him. It had been for Cam one of the very few victories that went some way to making up for months, years even, of defeats.

Cam looked out of the window and saw that the snow had already stopped. The little that had fallen was already beginning to melt; by morning there would be no memory of it on the ground. The logs he had put on the fire were more or less burnt out, and the room was turning cold and grey as ash. He put the guard on the fire and went softly upstairs, his feet making no sound at all; he knew those stairs so well, knew each tread that squeaked, as though an unwritten map of them lay in his head. Would he have begun to forget all the details of home, he wondered, before he returned?

He went to bed, but although he was dog tired he didn't sleep for a long time; he seemed to be always on the edge of it but half-thinking, half-dreaming. In his mind he kept hearing what he thought were curlews crying, although he knew it was not the time for them; some old story came back to him that the crying was a mourning for loves lost long ago. And it seemed to be the name Rosie they were crying, until gradually they seemed to go further and further away and he lost them altogether…

'Is it breakfast or lunch you're wanting?' his mother said with a twinkle as Cam eventually lumbered blearily into the kitchen. 'You're certainly practising for your student days, I can see!'

'I have to finish my packing today,' Cam said as though it was a promise. 'Where're Dad and Rob?'

'Mending one of the fences. One of the sheep got tangled and made a right mess of the thing,' she replied. And then added: 'Was it a good ceilidh then? There was enough noise from you all anyway – I don't think I slept till about four.'

Before Cam had finished eating, his dad came in and announced that the fence was done.

'Come out when you're ready, Cam,' he said, changed into another pair of boots and disappeared upstairs. The boy was not sure what he meant, but he finished his breakfast and put on his boots and an anorak. By now the rain was coming down in earnest and the fields, when Cam looked out, were enveloped in mist.

Duncan came downstairs and they went out together to the barn. There were bales of hay stacked in the far corner; one of the new calves was tramping about its pen in the semi-darkness. After a few moments Cam's eyes became adapted to the gloom; he picked out the huge stack of logs over to the left that were ready for the winter, and the old implements from Toberdubh hanging now from nails in the stone walls. Then he saw it – there at their feet the harp was lying, cleaned now and beautiful, as if it had been made the day before. Cam looked at it with awe; he bent down involuntarily to touch it, stretching out reverent hands to feel the strings, to run his fingers gently over the wood, with the strange curling designs woven into it. It had been so lovingly restored by his father, polished so that the wood shone – no wonder he was looking so proud and glad, smiling at Cam. And then:

'I want you to have it, Cam,' he said quietly. 'There's plenty Rob'll get from here, but somehow I reckon this will mean more to you. As long as you don't go and sell it!' he added with a laugh.

'Oh dad, thanks...thanks so much.' He looked up at his father, overcome, grateful beyond words, but not sure. Rob wouldn't like it, he knew; Cam was not certain that it was the right thing for him to accept. Yet he did not want to hurt his father by saying no. He was silent for a moment. Then, 'It's amazing,' he said, running his hand again over the shining wood. 'I just wish Richard could've seen it, you know. Anyway, don't worry, I'll look after it all right!'

'Are you wanting those sheep brought in from the lower field?'

The two of them turned round in surprise at the sound of Rob's voice. He was standing there in the entrance to the barn; maybe indeed he had been there all along. Cam's heart hammered in his chest. He got up at once while Duncan Mackay began to tell his older son what he wanted done, and Rob started towards the house. Even by the way he walked, Cam was somehow sure that he had heard, sure too that he was angry and hurt by what his father had done.

'Rob!' Cam called lamely as they came back to the house, but his brother stormed inside, kicked off his muddy boots and banged away through the kitchen and upstairs. Morag Mackay turned round from the stove, her face full of questions; Cam didn't stop but followed Rob up to his room.

'Let me tell you this,' Rob said harshly, 'Dad can give you

whatever he wants but he can't give you Ardnish, see? This place is going to belong to me and there isn't a thing you can do about it. Once you've been to your nice little university you can go off and find some high-powered job somewhere and you'll soon forget this place ever existed. Anyway, you'd better, 'cos you won't be coming back here!' Incensed now, he made a grab for Cam's shoulder, but the boy ripped himself desperately from his grasp.

'Just leave me alone!' he found himself wailing as he escaped through the doorway and went battering back down the stairs.

'Cam?' said his mother anxiously as he went storming through the kitchen. 'Cam, what on earth is going on?'

But he didn't answer; he wouldn't stop, but pulled on his boots at speed and ran out of the door and on up to the path heading for the larch wood. His father caught sight of him from the barn and knew at once that something was wrong; he went back into the house to find out what it might be.

On Cam went at high speed until he reached the cover of the larch wood. He hoped his mother had not seen that he was crying; now he stopped and wondered what he should do. The rain was not as heavy as it had been, but fine now, like soft down. Every inch of the land was green and shining; the trees loomed out of the low mist and it seemed as if the whole world had been wrapped in cotton wool. As soon as he sat down on his favourite flat rock in the wood Cam let himself cry in earnest. He cried in anger and bewilderment, but above all because of the sheer injustice of it all. What had he done, after all? Why should Rob try to punish him for something which was not in the least his fault? It simply wasn't fair! But he was crying too because he loved Ardnish and it was a thought too terrible for words that he would be kept from his own home. This land was where everyone would be buried! All the ones who mattered to him. And he wasn't just thinking of their bodies – he meant their stories, their laughter, their lives! It was as though Rob meant to put up some huge electric fence around his beloved Ardnish to keep him out. It was unfair, it was unfair! Surely he couldn't mean it? But then, what would be the point of coming back if his brother hated him that much? How could he ever be happy here like that? Once his parents were dead, Rob would be master here and no longer afraid of what he could say or do.

He thought of himself in Aberdeen, watching from a window

the slush of traffic through grey streets, knowing that he could not go back, that he was a prisoner of the city. Surely Rob had no right to do such a thing to him! Yet the worst of it was that he knew deep in his heart that his brother would indeed have that right one day, that there was nothing at all he could do to stop him.

Cam got up from where he was sitting and began running again, not knowing why, but feeling he could not bear to sit still any longer. He did not want to see Ardnish, that much he knew; he could not bear to see it at this moment. He crashed through the trees and into the glade he had loved so much as a child and for a second he remembered the horseman, he was the horseman, ploughing on madly without any thought or care about where he was going. Abruptly he broke out on the other side of the wood, and in the bad light did not see the bank dipping away beneath his feet. Down he went, and hard over on his ankle; he gave a single cry as he landed and lay on the muddy bank, his hands splayed out behind him. For a second he did not move; he was too shocked to do anything. Then he shivered and tried to move his ankle, to raise himself, but pain at once jagged through his whole leg.

Now he wept again, for Ardnish, but also for his own misery; he wept because he felt as helpless as a child. The wind chilled him as it whipped round from the edge of the trees. At last he picked himself up carefully from where he lay and crouched over in a ball in an attempt to keep warm. The pain that seared through his ankle when he so much as twitched it seemed unbearable; he felt he dared not risk trying to walk. But what was he to do? The tears came again as waves of self-pity washed over him. His father would come to look for him in the end, he felt sure, once they all realised he had not returned. He wanted to be found and he did not. He was not sure any more what he really wanted. As he lay there miserably, rain lashed down and wind whirled through the larches; he closed his eyes and shivered.

Into his mind there came a picture from childhood. It was of a father standing outside a house with his arms thrown open wide, while a younger man, his son, toiled towards him from far away. The picture had been strange and wonderful all at once, filled with the bright colour of fruit and the hot light of a distant country. It came from a book his mother used to read to them of the story of the prodigal son. Then he thought about himself again – was he one who would go away and squander his inheritance in the city, he wondered bitterly? He might just as well, perhaps, for there would be no forgiveness or welcome home for him once his father had gone! He fell for a moment into the frame of that picture and saw himself running over the dusty track, there under the hot blue skies; but the doorway was blocked by the figure of his brother, and there was neither mercy nor love in his eyes.

'You won't come back here!' He heard Rob's words over and over again in his mind; each time he flinched from them. They were like a physical blow to him. If only, if only his father had never said anything about the harp! It had been that which sparked off the whole thing. His father had found the harp; it was his, and he had no wish to fight over it with his brother. But the quarrel was, he knew, about far more than that; it was about the land itself; it was about pride and honour and rights. There was something in him that was jealous all right, he had to admit that; he wished he had been the elder brother. But there was no way on earth the two of them could have shared Ardnish, no matter the number of its acres.

Maybe he should have been glad he was leaving, washing his hands of the whole sad quarrel for ever. Yet somehow that was not what he felt in his heart; that was no real answer, else he would not have wept so bitterly over Rob's harsh words – nor ended up here in the mud! The truth was that he had no heart to fight; it was not the way he wanted things at all.

The cold became worse as the wind blew in from the moor with another fierce barrage of rain. He must somehow manage to move into shelter or he'd be soaked to the skin in no time. He began to drag himself along, using his hands to propel himself, up the bank and into the shelter of the first of the trees. They splattered great heavy drops from their branches, but right up against one heavy trunk he was protected from the worst of the new rain. It was strangely warm too, he noticed, and he was reminded that it had been the same on the night he had tramped wearily back from Toberdubh with his father.

It was for just the very briefest moment that Cam saw the figure, so brief that he would never be sure whether his eyes had played a trick on him, or that it was all a figment of his imagination. For just that second, away over on the far side of the path something caught his eye, a flash of silver and a raised axe, the small dark man with the cloth about his shoulders. The really odd thing was that although the man was striking at the tree, his eyes did not seem to be on the blow; instead Cam had the queerest feeling that their eyes met, just for a brief second. And then nothing; Cam was left peering though the sheer grey curtain and the larches, seeing nothing but their dismal shadows and the white slicing of the raindrops. He was startled, but the thought of fear had never crossed his mind; that was what seemed so weird. It had happened so fast that he had had no time to think of being scared. But maybe it was because he had had no feeling of having seen a stranger. The man had been grey, etched as it were out of flint, ancient as the peat itself; Cam was sure of that. He was surely one of the first folk, the new breakers of the land who had come after the ice slid back and the earth warmed. He had been the first to make fields out of soil that had previously only grown trees. Yet there had been in him something of the look of Duncan Mackay – even of Cameron Mackay! It seemed such a stupid notion, one which he would never dare to say to anybody, and yet that had been his immediate thought as he caught sight of that face. Maybe it was because he had been thinking at that moment of his father; maybe it had all been imagination, a trick of the eyes, of the light? All the same, this wood held something of strangeness; he could never quite forget the horseman, and maybe other shadowy figures too, half-remembered from distant days of childhood – or from dreams? It was as if a curtain of time slid back now and then to a place between the worlds, where the people who had once stood there came back and were for a brief moment etched again.

He thought and thought about the flint man, and the more he did the more he felt him to have been their own ancestor, the very first one, perhaps, to name Ardnish, to mark its fields. He shuddered again at the strangeness of it and felt suddenly afraid and lonely; he did not want to look back there again in case the apparition should return.

He shifted his foot and it hurt so badly that he gave a moan in frustration and despair. The tears welled in his eyes and the trees blurred into grey mist. He longed to go home, but home seemed to be the one place he could not go. Perhaps it was a long time after that, or perhaps it was hardly any time at all that Cam heard the sharp crack of a stick, and looked up startled to see a dark figure coming through the trees, jumping over the rocks at the side of the pool and walking up the path towards him.

'I'm here!' he called feebly from where he crouched under the larch, and the figure stopped, turned round and then spotted him and came up close. Their eyes met. It was Rob.

9

Strange that it should have been his brother who helped him back to the farm – strange, and more than a little uncomfortable. Cam felt strongly that he didn't want to be that close to him, to have to lean on his shoulder like that. Already, many times over, he felt himself to be the weak one, the inferior; it certainly needed no reinforcing! The two of them spoke little on the way back, nothing at least that did not have to do with the immediate business of getting back to Ardnish. The mist was rolling in again as they came slowly and drunkenly out of the shelter of the larches; Cam could see the white rolls of cloud driving in from the sea, so that even the bottom field was smudged and unclear now, on the edge of fantasy.

Every time he felt himself in danger of crying out with the pain of his ankle he bit his lip, closed his eyes and uttered not a word. It was as much as his life was worth, he decided, to make the slightest fuss about it. At any rate his pride was at stake.

He reckoned his parents must have sent Rob out to look for him. That must mean that the whole affair had come out before he left the house; he thought of this with a certain grim satisfaction. Most of the time, he knew, they took his side, and if Rob had been honest about his side of the story, Cam had no doubt his dad would have been wild as a bull about the whole thing.

'Out there and don't bother coming back until you've found him!'

Cam could well imagine the scene that had probably taken place; it wasn't often that Duncan Mackay got mad, but that was just the sort of thing he hated. And on the rare occasions when he and Rob fell out, they did it in style.

It was all very well, though, being satisfied that Rob had probably been drummed out of the house to find his brother, but it did nothing to heal the rift between them. If anything, Cam thought miserably as he hobbled the last yards to Ardnish and went inside, Rob would be all the more bitter with all the world against him. The warmth of the kitchen hit him at once and he realised how cold he was.

'Away upstairs and get that foot washed!' Duncan Mackay scraped back his chair and got up from the table, taking in the situation at a glance. 'See his heater's on in his room, Robert, and then come down here. Your mother's away into Findale.'

He winked at Cam as he went past him to the door and thumped a kindly hand on his shoulder. Things were pretty well just as he'd imagined they would be, thought Cam; he could hardly help but smile. Negotiating the steps up to his room was a nightmare, and he imagined he must have bitten off about half his tongue by the time they made it to the landing, but he survived.

'I doubt they'll amputate,' Rob suddenly said at Cam's door and shot a glance at him, his eyes sparkling for a second. Then he went ahead of Cam into the room, got the heater on and the curtains closed, and one of the bedside lights switched on. He then came back and helped his brother over till Cam collapsed a little melodramatically on to the bed. The rain was hammering like nails against the window. Cam half-expected Rob to turn and go at once, glad that his duty was over. But instead he squatted by the side of the bed all of a sudden, looking at his finger nails, not at Cam, frowning uncertainly.

'I'm sorry about what I said to you earlier,' he said in a rush. 'I didn't mean most of it – you know that.'

Cam looked up sharply from where he was lying, taken altogether by surprise, his heart beginning to throb in his chest with the shock of what Rob was saying. It hadn't been like this...

'Maybe it's just that Dad's so often on your side,' his brother continued, still not looking at him. 'Mum as well – I feel I'm always somehow on the outside. And you're the one who's going to university; you were always the one who did well at school. I dunno, maybe I feel this place is all I've got – the thought that one day I'll be able to farm it, do it as I want...'

His voice trailed away and he moved, uncomfortable as he was on the floor, still never looking at Cam but clearly thinking, thinking hard. His brother's heart was still racing sixteen to the dozen, his head quite dizzy with the sudden strange turn of events;

it was so unexpected. He wanted desperately to say something, to show that he was really listening and that what Rob was saying mattered, mattered indeed more than he could say. But his mouth was dry and he just sat and looked at Rob, dazed – like a stuffed goldfish; that was what Rosie would once have said.

'I always felt a complete failure,' he managed at last, shifting on the bed. 'I was always really jealous, Rob, 'cos you were stronger than me, you could do everything better round here, and you were popular... School and stuff, well, that was different; it never meant that much to me. I don't even know if I want to go away, to tell you the truth!'

Rob sniffed and looked up at that, and the two of them smiled.

'Maybe we were jealous of each other the whole way along,' Rob said quietly at last. 'Kind of stupid really, when you think about it. As Mum always says, life's too short as it is.'

They went quiet then, but Cam wanted to say something nonetheless, though he didn't know if the had the guts. It pounded in his head and he rehearsed it before daring to speak.

'About Ardnish, Rob. I know it'll be yours, of course, but...it means an awful lot to me, you know. I might...might need to come back. I...I just don't know what I want at the moment, what I may do in the future, but I love this place.'

Rob looked him full in the face now and then nodded, understanding in his eyes.

'I didn't mean what I said, right? All that was just rage, after I'd seen you and Dad in the barn, with the harp. D'you really think I'll be out with a shotgun, waiting for you to come off the main road, ready to blow your brains out?'

Cam giggled in spite of himself at the thought.

'Just because I'll be running this place doesn't mean you can't come back; get that into your head! There's no way on earth we could share this place, but...it'll always be your home too, no matter what happens.'

Cam was so glad that he felt his eyes blurred with a sudden warmth.

'Thanks, Rob,' he said – and almost immediately regretted it, for his brother threw him a black look at once.

'Nothing to thank me for,' he muttered as he struggled to get up from the floor.

Cam could have kicked himself; of course he knew how Rob

would hate to be thanked for something like that. He tried at once to redeem the situation.

'Going down to Findale tonight?' he asked. Rob rolled his eyes and looked away.

'Not after the fool I made of myself on Saturday night! Annie won't speak to me in a hundred years. No, there's plenty to be done around here, after all the time and sweat I spent trying to find out where you'd run away to!'

He turned round and glowered at Cam in jest.

'I'll look in and see how you're doing later, then. I'm not carrying a big hulk like you down to dinner, I hope you realise that!'

They laughed and Cam was glad. He laughed because of Rob's joking words, but he laughed even more because he felt warm inside, because things were all right; they were healed. It would not always be like this; he knew that well enough. But somehow it didn't matter; what was important was here and now, and for that he was deeply grateful.

'By the way,' Rob said as he turned round at the door, in no real hurry to go, 'I wouldn't want that harp anyway – not after hearing that old story of grandpa's.'

Cam frowned, all the pain of his ankle forgotten.

'What story was that?'

'Och, come on, you must remember! I'm sure you must have been there too? It was one of those times we begged to stay up there at Toberdubh instead of coming back here at night. It worked a few times! The old man was trying to scare the daylights out of us with all sorts of stories about weird lights on Ben Luan, folk wandering off and never coming back – all that kind of thing.'

That story about Ben Luan was certainly clear enough in Cam's mind. Had this one been told too on the night that Rob was remembering? He couldn't think of it for the life of him.

Rob came back then and sat down at the end of the bed. He wasn't exactly one for telling stories, not this kind at any rate.

'Well,' he began, 'as far as I can recall it was all to do with the devil and the start of the world... Don't laugh at me, or I'll thump your ankle!'

'I'm not laughing!' Cam protested even although it wasn't exactly true. He was just happy; he was really wildly happy and he couldn't help himself.

'Anyway, according to grandpa, the whole floor of heaven is made of ice. Well one day the devil, who was at this time still a good angel, was walking away out on the edge of this ice, where nobody was supposed to go. He was carrying his harp with him and some kind of brand – a torch I suppose. Anyway, he got right to the edge in his pride and fell right through the ice, down, down the whole way to earth, till he landed up, according to grandpa, bang in the middle of that mound of earth out there, right between the two fields.'

Cam was smiling suspiciously at all this. Rob was far better at making up stories than he'd ever imagined. He raised his eyebrows but said not a word.

'I'm only telling you what I remember!' Rob protested. 'I'm not asking you to believe the whole thing! Anyway, I forgot to mention the brand. When the devil was falling out of the skies he let go of it and it landed somewhere away to the north, right in the middle of the ancient forest, and just about the whole of it was burned. At any rate, that's how the harp landed in the old mound there, and it's best left where it is, if you ask me...it's an instrument of darkness.'

Rob's voice ended in a melodramatic whisper and Cam laughed until it hurt.

'That last bit at least you added!' he said. 'Whatever else grandpa actually told, you put in that bit about the harp, Rob! Come off it!'

'I'm only repeating word for word the story I remember,' his brother countered innocently, standing up to go. It might have been that there was just the tiniest edge of a smile on his lips. 'If you don't want to believe me, that's up to you. But you have been warned...'

He looked round a last time from the door and showed the whites of his eyes. Then he disappeared.

Cam felt the silence after he had gone. Yet his sadness was gone as well; instead, he felt the warmth of the house about him, was aware in a new way of its security and peace. It was growing dark; he could see the edges of black between the curtains. He got up and struggled over to the window despite the pain of his foot.

At times on evenings like this he felt the strangest melancholy, as if the blackness itself came over his spirit, with mist clogging his chest, making it an effort for him to breathe. It was a nowhere time, this period between the end of summer and the beginning of winter, seemingly bleak and dead. Maybe these days were something that only Scotland could produce; perhaps the nature of the land itself, beneath these skies, added to the gloom.

Even tonight he felt the air stuffy, so he pushed up the window and a hint of the coldness of early evening came into the room. Almost at once he heard sounds, very muffled at first so that he was not quite certain what they were; perhaps Rob was out at the car, or something was being mended. They were like squeals, high-pitched and very far away, the intervals between them were so long sometimes that he felt that whatever was making them had gone. Yet now they came again and were closer; they seemed so near, just over the house maybe, that he had the feeling that he could have raised his arm into the darkness and touched their flight. For now he knew: they were wild geese – the first geese returning from Iceland after the long summer days.

A flood of childhood memories washed over him – so many nights when he had wakened up and heard a skein of them dragging overhead. They always made his heart leap, although he never quite understood why. As a child he had felt strongly that it was a terrible thing to shoot one of these wonderful birds which had toiled long and hard to reach this sanctuary of land after a perilous journey across the sea. Once, when he and Rob were very young, his father had gone out with a gun, and they had begged him not to shoot any; they had gone on badgering him until he had reluctantly lowered his gun and come slowly inside, resignation written all over his face. Cam still felt the same now; the geese were to be welcomed, of that he was absolutely sure. He had had no reason ever to change his mind.

Geese would often get lost on just such nights as this. Lone birds could be heard crying in distress above the rooftops, searching for a way back to join the rest of the flock; orphans deserted by their companions. The mist apparently caused their disorientation, destroying their vision as it swallowed up the land. Time after time, he would lie awake in the middle of the night, willing them to break free and escape, sharing in the distress he sensed in their cries. It would be like that tonight, he feared, if there were many coming in over the sea in the first wave of arrivals. And just for a moment he felt himself to be like one of them, wandering in a mist, not sure of the path ahead, struggling to hold on to faith in the face of uncertainty.

But now, as he waited by the window, a stronger breath of cool air came into the room; he saw that a wind had got up and was filling the trees, and he was glad, sure that by morning the last of the mist would have been blown away, and that the geese would be able to find their way back to their well-known haunts.

It comforted him to reflect that some things never really changed; if he were to go down now to his dad and ask him on what day the geese had come back for the past ten years or more, the reply would be that it was always the same. The same day of the same month, crossing the vastness of sea and land, to return to the same fields! It was as if there were unwritten cycles that were never broken but kept on, year after year. The living things that traced these cycles did not understand what they were fulfilling. Nor did they ever question them. Perhaps he was in his own cycle, far too big and strange for him to begin to understand, but one that he should not question, but learn to take on trust. Although it comforted him it also disturbed him, for if that were true, then how much freedom remained his own? It became too much for him to think through; he yawned, pulled down the window, shut out the mist and the voices of the geese, and hobbled back to bed. He did not want to think too much about anything; the day had been too long, too confused, already. His head was whirling as it was with all that had happened. He grimaced as he remembered that he was no farther on with his packing, and in a couple of days he was due to leave.

There was a rap on the door and his mother came in, a tray in her hands.

'Are you warm enough, Cam? We still haven't seen to that ankle of yours and you've been in for half an hour! I've made you some bacon and eggs.'

He smiled at her as she laid the tray on his lap and then went round the room making sure the heater was on, closing the curtains carefully where Rob had not bothered; she came back and sat on the very edge of the bed.

'Now I don't want to be nosy, Cam, but I just hope you and Robert have made up. It was silly of him to make you run off...'

'Mum, it's all right,' he interrupted gently. 'We got it sorted. And my foot'll be fine, don't worry. And thanks for bringing this up.'

'I remember doing it often enough for you when you were a wee boy,' she said. 'Those times when you would have an attack of asthma in the middle of the night, and one of us would come and read to you until you were better. I could always tell when that was, because you'd always ask for tea! I used to go down, feeling so relieved, to make you tea and toast.'

He smiled, remembering too, remembering small things. He used to have a huge bear sitting up on the dressing-table, and in the night when he was scared he could see its shadow and that comforted him. The times when he had had asthma during his childhood were all rolled into one now in his mind; he could clearly recall the terrible toil of trying to breathe in each time, as though he was climbing a sheer mountain. And the air he breathed never seemed to be enough; it was more like wool than anything else.

'Didn't you used to tell me stories too, mum?' he asked. 'I'm trying to remember.'

Morag smiled.

'I think there was only one, ever – you know I'm hopeless at that! But that one I used to tell you over and over again, desperate to take your mind off things. Poor wee soul, I don't think you ever minded; you were most likely too busy struggling to get better. Och, what was it now? Some silly thing about a boy going into a wood and finding a balloon, a basket balloon, and flying off to the end of the world...'

'That's it, I remember now! And wasn't there some old man in a tower?' said Cam.

'Aye, that's right,' his mother smiled. 'He found some magician at the very far north of the world in a white tower, and he could ask for just one wish...'

Cam nodded.

'I can remember my wish all right – I always just asked to get better! And I did in the end. I can't even remember the last time I had asthma. But it wasn't a silly story, Mum; it used to mean a lot to me.'

His mother said nothing, but her eyes were glad.

'Well, I won't be able to look after you once you're away in Aberdeen. I just hope you find good friends before too long, Cam; that'll make all the difference. Now I'm going to go away and leave you to eat. Then you should try and get a good sleep.'

She was mothering him again and normally he would have protested, pulled her up for treating him too much like a child, but this time he didn't. He thought of the many nights when she had given up her own nights' sleep for him, coming in to read when his breathing was bad or when he had been afraid. He thought of the long years he had been at home, and all he had taken for granted. Now was no time to rebel against that closeness and love; there would be time enough for the distance to come between them, all the weeks and months when he'd be away. These were last days for her – the end of one part of her life and the beginning of a new one. It was no easier for her to see him go than for him to leave.

'Thanks, Mum,' he said instead. 'I'm glad I'm here.'

She slipped out of the room putting the main light off as she left. He heard the television on downstairs, the laughter punctuating some programme like clockwork. Only two more nights would he be in this house. At that moment he did not want to be going anywhere; he would have been more than happy to remain and forget that his university place ever existed. He finally put the light out, even though it was still quite early and he was not really ready to sleep. At the back of his conscious thought was the muffled sound of the television, but in the end he didn't know if it was real or just his own imagination. He slowly drifted asleep, but not very deeply, so that when the noise came at the window he was not surprised, but looked up without fear to see what had made the sounds.

Although it was dark, the whole window shone silver with moonlight, and he knew that the mist had gone. He struggled out of bed but the strange thing was that he felt no pain at all in his foot. He looked out of the window and there below him he saw Richard, just as he had seen him on that last morning in the summer dawn.

'It's all right, I'm all right,' he kept saying, over and over again. 'You have to come with me, now! Climb out of the window!'

Cam wanted to speak but somehow he could not. He jumped down to the grass, and again he felt nothing in the foot he had hurt. Already Richard was gone; he was running away fast over the ground in the direction of the sea, and Cam ran after him; he ran like the wind. Away in the distance over the sloping ground he saw the weird hill, shaped like a barrow, with all the pine trees on its summit. Richard, he knew, had loved that place more than anywhere in the world, more even than he loved Shuan and the Camas shore on the far side. It was there he had found the hundreds of pigeon feathers lying under the trees: the place where the angels came to moult.

At last they reached it, Cam a bit later than his friend, and they stood on the summit. Richard didn't look at him; he was craning his neck to look right up above him at the skies.

'The northern lights!' he kept saying. 'Just look at the northern lights!'

So Cam looked up and saw the fires playing in the skies, leaping and chasing each other so fast that your eyes could not follow them.

'If you whistle they'll come to you!' Richard said. 'Didn't you know that? They're wild horses, not lights at all. You can ride them if you can catch them!'

Cam tried to whistle but no sound would come at all. He kept looking up and wishing he could, for it seemed the best thing he had ever heard. But when giving up at last, he looked around him, he saw that Richard was no longer there; he was running across the last fields towards Shuan, as fast as any horse, and he was growing fainter and fainter all the time.

Cam tried to call for him to come back; he opened his mouth in anguish; but it was too late, and the world went dark.

10

The next day passed uneventfully enough for the most part. Cam finally got down to the last of his packing, lugging things from the attic as best he was able with his bad ankle, sorting out the new piles of clothes his mother brought for him. Outside it was raining – the colour had drained away from everything – and the house was filled with a heavy, grey light. Rob stayed in his room most of the time, the walls thudding with his music; even Duncan had been forced indoors for much of the time, his mood seemingly as bleak as the weather. The rain chimed and sang, it came in at cracks and formed a pool on the pantry floor. Morag was busy with cloths, going here and there in a house that had its lights on all day, for the grey cloud was so heavy that it seemed the sun had vanished for ever.

By the time their midday meal was over Cam was sick of the whole business. Three huge cases and several bags stood ready on the floor of his room and he wanted no more of them. He banged down the stairs, clutching the banister for support, and went into the kitchen to find Misty and Fruin stretched out on the floor, and his parents at the table.

'I'm going out,' he announced, stroking Misty's forehead as she slept.

'You must be joking,' his father said. 'Have you looked out recently by any chance?'

'What about your foot, Cam?' added his mother anxiously. 'Do give it a chance – give it time to heal.' She left the letter she was writing and came over to stand beside him, her face full of concern.

'I'll be fine,' he smiled at them. 'I'm not going to get gangrene or anything like that! Anyway I just want to get out of the house, and my ankle's a whole lot better since Rob helped me to strap it up. I've almost finished my packing, believe it or not!'

Duncan returned to his newspaper and Morag accepted Cam's going once she had seen him wrapped up in his oilskin and he had assured her he'd survive a monsoon. She slipped a huge sandwich into his pocket, all the same.

'And here's a mug of tea before you go!'

He went out of the house and just stood in the porch for a moment, listening to the hiss and rattle of the rain. Thank goodness Rob had come up the track to the larch wood the night before or he would still be lying there feeling sorry for himself! He felt a bit of a fool now for having run away as he had done; the quarrel with Rob now seemed so far away, his fears of last night foolish and exaggerated.

He was keen to go down to Findale, if only his foot would allow him to reach that far. There was something he thought he might do there, and anyway the walk would clear his head after the hours of packing. He set off fairly slowly down the uneven farm track, still

84

wincing if he happened to hit the wrong side of a stone and pain shot through his ankle. The pools in the road were like liquid chocolate; he remembered so well coming along here with his mother when he was a child, Rob dragging at one hand and himself at the other, both wearing wellingtons and making the most of the chance to splash in the puddles as hard as they were able.

A few hundred yards along the track the rain suddenly came on heavier than ever. Cam looked back, his head hunched deep down into his oilskin and his hands buried in the pockets, seeing Ardnish lit like a honeycomb. For a second he felt lazy and toyed with the idea of turning back, but then he remembered his half-formed plan and felt this would be his last chance. He would go on. And if he kept up a good enough pace, he could be back before six.

He went on, still walking with care, until he reckoned he should be coming within sight of the gate and the main road. The mist was so thick that he could barely see twenty yards in front of him, so that even following the track was a trial at times. As he looked ahead and to his left, a boulder seemed to loom out of the grey, maybe one of the great chunks of stone left there when the track up to the farm was built. But as he watched he saw the thing move, and then another shape moved out of the mist, and he realised these were not boulders at all but the backs of stags and hinds.

He stopped stock still, becoming aware that he was now off the main artery of the track; he heard, rather than saw, the beasts in the poor light, heard the sound of many hooves clicking over the rocks then digging down into the marshy ground below. However, they weren't going away from him at all, but rather coming closer, shyly, their eyes wary and never still, lowering their heads and looking round, hinds and yearlings, and the stags with their full crowns of antlers further away at the back.

'Hallo there,' he said very gently. 'What d'you want then?'

He stretched out his hand warily, but too quickly, and there was a drumming as the nearest backed away in fear. Yet they were curious and came edging back, closer all the time; he wondered why they had come down so low this early in the year. There surely can't have been all that much snow on Ben Luan a couple of nights ago? It seemed unlikely that the cold had driven them down. He was really puzzled but forgot his questions when the nearest and bravest hind lowered her head so that she was only inches from his own face, her breath steaming up into the mist.

All of a sudden he recalled the sandwich his mother had stuffed into his pocket before he left the house; he'd had a mighty breakfast and hardly needed to worry about food for a long while yet. Very carefully he raised his hand to his pocket and managed to bring out the bag without a crackle. The wet noses strained in curiosity.

'Now, only one bit each,' he said sternly. 'Ladies first.'

The soft muzzles came one after another to take the pieces of bread he offered. Their mouths were like wet mushrooms, the kind found in the fields early in the morning following a night's rain. After a little he dared to reach up and stroke the hard fur on their foreheads; only one or two jerked back frightened. So they came eventually to form a warm ring round him, misty and faint on the edge of the thick mist, as the rain continued to drum down and a swollen burn crashed noisily beside them on its way to the river.

In the end they moved off, reluctantly and not in fear. Cam felt honoured, as if they had chosen him, trusted him. It was as though for a brief time there was no longer that sad gulf between the world of men and theirs, the wild kingdom. In the mist he seemed to have stumbled over a boundary into a place where fear and the gun did not belong, but perhaps that was only wishful thinking on his part. At last they were out of sight in the blanket of mist, and, but for the dampness on his palm, and the last crumbs of the sandwich, it might have been that they had never existed at all.

It seemed to take him ages to get back on to the main track. Because he was near the river and the woods, mist steamed even more densely into the air and with every yard it seemed harder to be sure of the way ahead. Once or twice he slipped on a deep rut of mud and his ankle throbbed with pain; he felt he would never reach the main road when all of a sudden a car slushed down quite near to him and he was there, only a mile from Findale.

The place he was aiming for was nearer than that, though. A long time ago, up on the hillside just outside Findale, and nearer for folk who came down from places like Ardnish and Toberdubh, there had been another church. At its back was a graveyard where the stones were very old; Cam used to think of them as being like an old man's teeth. But there were one or two fairly recent stones as well, despite the fact that Craig Church was now in a semi-ruined state and had held no religious services for close on fifty years.

It was a queer place really, steep above the road on the right-hand side, so high you could look out west from it and just glimpse the blue rim of the sea through the trees. You had the feeling that the place was much older than the grey kirk itself, which was probably young in comparison with whatever else had been built on that sharp rock.

Cam went along the main road at a reasonably fast pace once he had reached it. Sandy's dad passed him in a car, doing about fifty down the brae, but he screeched to a halt to ask if Cam wanted a lift into Findale. Cam just grinned and shook his head, then waved as the car shot off – far too fast for a day of mist, Cam decided – towards the village.

He got to the Craig and went through the rusty gate that protested creakily as he opened it. A huge black scatter of crows took off from the yews and rowans that grew around the hillock, reminding Cam of flecks of ash as they disappeared into the mist. The path was silver with water, indeed the entire hill was literally streaming with the rains of the past night and day, so that it took him all his time to reach the top and go round the back of the old church to the graveyard. A robin sitting on a wall looked at him, its head on one side, almost as though it had been employed to vet the visitors and couldn't quite make up its mind about Cam, who stopped and smiled as he looked at it.

'All right if I go in?' he said, but the robin darted away. He glanced over to his left, down and through the trees, but of course the sea was gone today, swallowed by the dense mist. He went on quickly, the faintest edge of fear in his heart, right up to the far left-hand corner...

RICHARD BRENNAN

The stone was small and simple, and there were new flowers there – his mother never failed. Cam wasn't sure why they had chosen this place rather than the regular graveyard down at Findale; perhaps it was because they could come here more often and remain undisturbed. Or perhaps because it was within sight of the sea, and Richard had loved that more than anything.

Cam crouched down and felt strange; there was no feeling that Richard was here as there was out at Camas, or at the barrow hill.

He lowered his eyes and shivered as the rain came down harder than ever.

'I'll be back,' he whispered, feeling all the same that he was talking to himself. 'I'm going away, but it won't be forever, for plenty of reasons. I won't forget.'

He straightened up and looked round somewhat furtively, afraid lest anyone else might have come in behind him and overhear.

Then he thought of something and went back towards the gate for a moment. There were pigeons up in the trees, and as he came out on to the path they fluttered away with a grey whirring. There on the ground, sure enough, were some feathers, and Cam smiled to himself as he gathered up the very whitest he could find and turned back again, shutting the gate behind them. He laid the feathers carefully in front of the grave, his mind going back to that day with Richard long ago and the strange ancient hill.

'I hope the angels come here too,' he said, and turned away for a last time.

He had intended going back to Ardnish after that, but he didn't. He was wet as it was and his foot was bearing up better than he had expected, so instead he headed down into Findale. Rain came in huge drops from the trees on each side of the road and he walked hunched up – like a dwarf – to avoid the splashes from the branches. The river seemed to be growling like a dog at the end of a leash; through the grey light he could see it well enough, leaping down in white curves in its final run to the sea. Everything was glassy and shiny, rhododendrons massed on one side of the road, mist coming like steam through the foliage.

Cam came into the village, over the bridge and into the main street. He took a look through the window into the public bar at the Arms; there was only one man inside with his elbows folded on the counter, slumped over his beer. The place seemed warm and alluring and Cam looked longingly at the roaring fire in the big stone fireplace which cast a warm glow over the room. He wished he could go in; then he thought of Rob, and the whole saga of last Saturday night – if by any chance Annie came in, he would have no idea what to say to her. He turned and went on.

Without thinking he found himself going up Sinclair Street and smiled; this was the way to Rosie's house, at one time so familiar. How many times had he begged his dad to take him down here on a Saturday to visit her, his heart thumping with excitement! It was mad to come here now, but still he went on; he was wandering without thinking and he carried on right to her house, which was the last on the left-hand side.

Her room was round the side, but she was sure to be out; he walked quietly up the driveway, seeing no sign of life from the house. To his surprise he saw a faint glimmer of light from her window and heard the thud of music – she must be up there after all! He stayed, watching, rooted to the spot as he thought back to the days in the past when he had come here... The times they had hidden behind a bush in the garden and kissed, the times they had climbed into a tree and annoyed the neighbour's dog, the time they had thought a cloud was a flying saucer, the time they had fished a goldfish out of the pond... Then there was movement up above and he awoke out of his reverie, scared that someone might come out on to the porch and find him here like this.

All the same, he didn't want to go away without saying goodbye. He had loved her once, and there was an empty place inside him now because of that. It would do no harm. Cam bent down and picked up a chip of stone and chucked it up at the window. His aim was good enough but it only glanced against the pane and clicked down again on to the drive. The second hit the glass properly and startled him; he waited for the window to be pushed up but as he held his breath there was nothing, only the beat of the music and the steady rain. He turned to go; the idea had been daft in the first place... The noise of the window going up made him jump; there she was, leaning out now with the glow of a cigarette in her hand, searching the semi-darkness to see who was there.

'Hi, Rosie, it's me, Cam! Did I scare you?'

'Cam you nearly gave me a heart attack, that's all!'

She turned round into the room for a second and screamed for the music to be turned down.

'Liz and Jenny are here for the night. My folks are away in Fort William. Are you coming in? C'mon, there's heaps to drink!'

He heard screams of laughter in the background and wished heartily that he hadn't bothered coming; but it was too late.

'No thanks, I'd better get back before it gets too dark. All the best for your course, though, Rosie – I hope you get on well.'

Already he was beginning to move away. Now there was a confusion of folk at the window and another gale of raucous laughter. Somebody wolf-whistled.

'See you then, Cam!'

'Yeah, see you,' he answered, and knew in his heart he didn't mean it. Cam the boy and Rosie the girl were dead, in a way as dead as Richard. All that was left was a garden deep inside his head and pictures – a whole lot of pictures that were faded like those in an old album. Now it was closed, but there were fresh pages in his hands, photographs that had not yet been taken. These were the ones that mattered now, he thought; these were the ones he should treasure.

Limping, he reached the main road through Findale and suddenly felt overwhelmingly tired. He wished he had had the good sense to turn back after going up to the graveyard; he would have been home by now. Slowly he made his way to the old bridge and leaned over it, listening to the loud crash of the swollen river as it tumbled in white falls over the rocks on its way to the sea. He would go on Wednesday he decided. There was no point in putting it off any longer; he had piles of books to buy for the start of term and plenty of things to organise. It seemed like a weight on his shoulders; he stood up, sighed, and resigned himself to the long walk home, hoping his ankle would stand it. A car was edging its way along the side of the road; in its lights the rain lashed down at an angle. He wondered for a moment if someone was about to ask the way. By the time he reached it he realised it was their own car and saw Rob behind the wheel.

'Your mother was worried about you,' Rob said dryly, rolling the window down. 'She was sure you'd get frostbite and die all alone on the moor.' He opened the passenger door and Cam saw that there was a hint of a smile on his face.

They hardly talked on the way home, but it wasn't a jagged kind of silence as it might have been, Cam thought gratefully; not the sort of silence there used to be so often between them after a row. This was more of a contented silence, a companionship which did not need any words.

The car went splashing through the flooded parts of the road but Rob didn't drive fast, not as he would have done if Annie had been in the car. Cam was content to sit and look out into the darkness. He was tired and his ankle was strummed by pain; he was glad he hadn't had to face the whole walk back. He listened to the thudding of the windscreen wipers and sleepily half-closed his eyes until the lights of Ardnish stabbed him awake.

Despite his tiredness he did not go early to bed. Instead he repacked one of his cases, found an old box of letters and sat for ages reading them. Rob and his father were talking downstairs about some new building or other; Cam heard snatches of the conversation in between finding things of interest from the past. There were several letters from Richard dating back to a time when the Brennans had gone down to England for an entire summer. He wondered whether he should keep them; in the end he stuffed all of them back into the box; they were still precious in their own way, with stories in them that he did not want to forget.

After a while he heard his father coming upstairs and only Rob remained in the kitchen. Cam felt cold in his room and went down, calling goodnight to his parents who were talking softly in the next room.

'So when're you away?' asked Rob, turning round from where he was sitting at the table.

'Och, Wednesday morning, if anyone'll be so kind as to take me to the station.'

'I doubt it'll be a problem,' Rob said severely, 'that 'phone has been ringing all evening with volunteers. No, I'll probably be able to take you myself; it will get me out of here for a bit. Have you much stuff?'

Rob sat till eleven, then banged around the house looking for this and that before finally going up to bed. Cam still sat by the fire, his feet cushioned by the black and white curve of Fruin. He was in a pensive mood and for some reason his thoughts tonight kept returning to Cameron Mackay, his grandfather, and especially to the final days he had spent in this house before his death. Sometimes, as now, Cam found himself wishing fervently that he had asked him more about the old days, about how it had been to live at Toberdubh after the war. How many stories were left for him some day to pass on to his own children? Precious few; if only he had thought while there was still time! Those memories were of great value, like flecks of gold panned from a river. But he had lost his chance. His grandfather had always been there, as familiar and seemingly as permanent as the single pine tree that had stood out on the moor beside the old house at Toberdubh. But the tree had been blown down in a storm, and all that was left of it was a few poor branches.

Cam pulled down the radio from its shelf and stood it on the floor beside him. Somehow he wanted to hear human voices; he felt the oppressive silence of the house; he was aware of the intensity of the night outside with the mist, miles and miles of it. It seemed as if Ardnish was the only thing alive in the darkness; out of every window there was nothing but blackness. He clicked on the radio and rolled the dial on and on. There were sudden flickers of language – a woman speaking German with such clarity that she could have been sitting in the room with him, a French song, a report in a language which he thought was probably Russian, something else that came and went in waves which in the end he recognised as Spanish. Then a very precise voice told him, in English, that it was a quarter to twelve.

There were all these languages, but there was no Gaelic. It had never occurred to him before, but now the thought of it made him really angry. In all of the darkness out there he couldn't hear so much as a word of Gaelic! And yet up there to his right was Toberdubh; farther over was Crossallan, and out ahead of him the Hebrides – all of them places that had at one time been filled with the sound of Gaelic. It was as if his grandfather and his like had been shut out, pushed away and forgotten by the modern world.

He put the radio away and went to look out of the window again. In the darkness he could clearly hear new skeins of geese coming in across the land. They triumphed over the dark! He pulled open the back door and stood there in the light, straining upwards to listen to their voices. They would come back; year after year they would come back, no matter how many guns tried to blast them from the skies. And maybe, too, the language would survive, maybe it would come back before it was too late. If it did not it would be a death, like the death of his own grandfather. He saw him now as he had been in weakness during his last days in the house; in him was a language and a way of life, both dying with him. And he was suddenly aware of how precious and fragile life was.

11

During the night the weather cleared. The rain stopped a little after midnight and the clouds drove inland, for all the world like great chariots or the ramparts of castles. The wind went too, all of a sudden, so it was dead still, as if the land held its breath. Stars crackled overhead; the grass stems became edged with frost diamonds so that they looked like jewelled swords. And out of nowhere the moon came, a wobbling shape like a balloon filled with water, very pale at first. The stags and hinds looked up towards Ben Luan, their eyes filled with gold, but then they took off across the moors, their brittle hooves clicking against the stones; the only other sound was of rushing, as the water in the full burns careered from the shoulders of the hills, white and foaming. The sheep lay close into the dykes, their fleeces long now and ready for the hard bite of winter ahead; they were like boulders in the lee of the rocks.

And in the sturdy house of Ardnish the people slept. The work of autumn was almost done; what remained was to tie up and secure all that was precious against the onslaught of the winter storms which would surely come. The house lay dark and small beneath the moors, like some sleeping wildcat with its eyes shut.

Out at the back, in the old barn that smelled of hay and dung and dust, the moonlight fell through the thick beards of cobwebs that muzzled the windows, down across the ancient harp that lay against the wall. At times, as the beams shifted, it was almost as if invisible hands lifted again and played the strings that had been silent for perhaps a thousand years.

'Ca-am! Come on, Cam, wake up!'

He moaned his way out of deep sleep and dragged himself awake. Somewhere up in the grey light was the face of his father. Why did he have the conviction that it was only about half-past six?

'It's a grand morning. Thought we might take a walk over to Toberdubh, Cam. I'll go down and make a cup of tea.'

Cam was still unable to put a whole sentence together, but his face spoke volumes. He looked at his father with such anguish that Duncan, afraid he might burst out laughing, went over and pulled back the curtains, remembering how Cam, even as a little boy, had always hated getting up in the mornings. Steel blue light flooded the room as Cam sat up at last, shivering in the room's cold. He tried to dig up the memory of the previous night and recalled the pelting rain. How was it possible? He shuffled over to the window and looked with wonder at the sharp blades of sunlight scything the fields, diamonds glittering on the grass and a white frost like the breath of an ice dragon. Below in the kitchen he heard his father singing something unbelievably cheery. With very bad grace he pulled on old clothes and stumbled downstairs.

'Are you all ready for tomorrow?' his father asked when they were at the table. Cam nodded, his hands clasped round the hot mug as he drank his tea.

Outside, the ground was rutted with frost. The cold hit Cam's face like a slammed door, his eyes ran and his nose felt pinched. There was ice by the back of the barn, ice that squeaked as their boots passed over it. Somewhere very high up there was yet another arrowhead of geese; Cam could hear their faint cries, but although he searched the skies above he could see nothing.

Wisely his father gave him time to become human again; he walked with an easy stride a few steps ahead as they climbed to the level of the larches and began the walk through the wood, golden in its autumn colours. His father knew well that if you began talking to Cam too early in the morning you might easily have an argument on your hands.

At last they reached the far side of the wood and began the trek over the moor. They walked together now, both with hands buried in the pockets of their anoraks. Cam was barely an inch shorter than his father; he would be taller yet. Duncan put a hand on his son's shoulder and pointed up into the sky.

'Hen harrier,' he said, as a pale-coloured hawk took off from the heather and began crossing the hilly country on slow and regal wings. Cam was impressed.

'Wouldn't have noticed,' he admitted.

'Reminds me of a time I was up in Sutherland,' Duncan said suddenly. 'I may have been there with my father – aye, that's right; we were spending a couple of weeks on the coast in the summer, staying with a cousin of his. Anyway, this day he and I were going out over the moors and it was blazing hot and very hard going. I think I'd gone for a swim in one of the hill lochs (there's about as much water as land there) and we were on our way home. Well, this big man popped out of the heather and he was like a cartoon character – you know, tweed coat and trousers, huge general's moustache, gun under his arm. Just glared at us with flaming eyes and shouted, "Get off my land!"'

'What did your dad say?' asked Cam.

'Well, that was the great thing. I can still remember being scared out of my wits, but he just took my hand and somehow that made me feel braver. He simply looked steadily at the man for a minute, holding his gaze. Then he said very quietly: "I'm not going anywhere." The man looked as though he'd burst a blood vessel any minute; his face was purple. Then your grandfather went on: "My people were Mackays. They were thrown off this land once – their own land. But I'm not going to be. I believe I have more right to be here than you have." And he walked straight on with me, head held high, not proud, just keeping his dignity. Left the man spluttering, raging his head off, but he never looked back once!'

'Brilliant!' said Cam, smashing an ice-covered pool with evident satisfaction under his foot. They chuckled happily to themselves until they had passed the pine tree and were within sight of the chimneys of Toberdubh. The boy was warm and at last fully awake and he felt good; he felt strong and suddenly happier than he had done for days. He just wished that on a morning like this Cameron Mackay were still alive and that they were about to see him. He wished it so fervently that the back of his eyes burned, and he couldn't answer his father when he turned to him and asked him something about the key of the house.

'You still miss him?' Duncan asked unexpectedly as they stood at the door. All Cam could manage was a nod; he felt a fool as he fought his tears.

'I miss him too,' said his father as they went in to the cold of the sitting-room and smelled the edge of dampness there; the dark silence. Duncan said no more but searched for matches and lit the old paraffin stove. Their breath fogged the room.

'I wanted to bring you here for a reason, Cam,' Duncan said. 'This land is yours too; never be afraid of standing for it. I'm a

95

fortunate man having you and Rob to follow me – most of the young folk in the Highlands today can't wait to get away. Just look at Rosie, the girl you were so fond of – they're all bored stupid in the country and desperate to be away in the city. I'm glad, and very grateful, you're not like that. Oh, I know you're going to university in Aberdeen; I understand that all right, but what I'm saying is, don't ever be afraid of coming home.'

There was a knot in Cam's throat and he couldn't say a thing. He just nodded, feeling as if a heavy sack had just been lifted from his shoulders.

'It can take long enough to know exactly what you want,' his father went on. 'Maybe you'll find it in the city, but maybe you won't, and there's no shame in coming to a point when you say you were wrong. I know fine how torn you are about leaving Ardnish, Cam. Rob knows it too. But don't think any of us feels we're saying goodbye to you forever. There's next autumn's tatties to be done, for one thing,' he added with a wink.

They stayed in the house for a short time; then Duncan decided it was time he was getting back to his work. At the back door, Cam looked up at Ben Luan and he hardly remembered ever having seen it so sharp and clear, a grey pyramid with its granite slabs shining eerily in the steely light, standing out majestically against the brown of the moor. You could see so far that morning that Cam thought he might have glimpsed an eagle flowing through the blue skies half a mile up, or perhaps a flicker of deer. And then he recalled the strange happening of the day before, when for some reason the shy beasts had seemed to lose their fear of him; he would never understand either why they had been so low down at that time! His reverie was interrupted by his father, turning the key in the lock and saying quietly:

'You could always have this place, you know. Rob will have Ardnish all right, but if you were willing to take on Toberdubh you could have it and welcome. At least you know that.' He began to move away, swinging the key up and putting it in his pocket.

Cam felt overwhelmed.

'It means an awful lot to me, Dad,' he said at once, meeting his gaze. 'I can't tell you how much. Just to know it's there for me. I keep wanting...keep wanting to go and not wanting to go.'

His father smiled and ruffled his hair.

'That's been the story of this country since the beginning of time,' he said.

Together they started back to Ardnish.

The big cases stood near the front door, along with a little bundle of extra things that had been forgotten.

It had been a big meal, a memorable meal and Cam's favourite, and Morag Mackay had fluttered about the kitchen serving and clearing, her face white and drawn. Cam saw clearly what lay behind her eyes and wished he hadn't been so hard on her in these past days, that he could have sensed earlier her pain in letting him go.

For this special occasion there was wine on the table and Rob and his father were in hilarious mood, roaring with laughter over some story about a Dutch landowner over at Crossallan. Cam hadn't seen his brother so cheerful for a long time; he hoped that perhaps he was beginning to get over Annie at last, and that he wouldn't pursue her any longer after all that had happened.

They finished their meal and pushed the chairs back from the table. The kitchen was still warm after the hours of sunshine that had been pouring in the whole day. The sun was almost gone now, an orange bonfire blazing through the trees above Findale. It would be some view from the top of Ben Luan, Cam thought, and for one crazy moment he actually wondered whether he could go and climb the hill and be back in time to leave with Rob in the morning. But he knew that his ankle still flickered with pain if he happened to put too much weight on the one side, and if he were to fall on a shoulder of the Ben at this stage...

'Don't go and sleep in, now,' his brother said, punching him in the stomach. 'I'm up at quarter to six, so down here no later than half-past, sleepy head! I've got stuff to see to upstairs. See you in the morning.'

Three friends rang up after dinner to wish Cam all the best and remind him to work hard. He felt a bit as he had once done while waiting for a piano examination – a pit in his stomach, a kind of emptiness, a fear of what his new world would be like. He saw himself running up ancient stone steps, books and folders under his arms as groups of students moved towards doorways and towers. What if all of it was beyond him? Butterflies invaded his stomach and he felt his heart panicking. Deliberately he calmed himself; after all, even if all of it went terribly wrong, even if it turned out a total disaster, he could still come back; his father had said so. He didn't want it to be like that; after all the hard work and all the waiting, he really wanted to succeed.

'I've made you up a packed lunch,' his mother said, taking him out to where his cases waited and presenting him with a folded plastic bag.

'Mum, I haven't an inch of room,' he whined at first, and then hating himself, thanked her for it and stowed it away as best he could. He would look like a pack animal arriving in Aberdeen. Better make up his mind to face the expense of a taxi.

'Well, don't stay up too late tonight,' Duncan told him and put out the main light. His mother came over and hugged him hard for a long moment.

'See you in the morning,' she whispered.

He nodded, feeling a hard knot in his own throat. For a time he crouched by the fire, fighting for a place beside Fruin. The room had gone cold after the sun's dying and he chucked another log on the fire so that the flames leapt up like hungry wolves at the dry wood.

'I'll miss you, Fruin,' he said as he rumpled the collie's glossy black and white back; the dog stretched and yawned. 'Wish you could come with me, but you'd hate it – there isn't a sheep within miles!'

Once he was warmer he went over to his father's old desk in the corner and sat there. Maybe he should stay longer; he still didn't feel ready. The time had passed so quickly! Yet what more was there to do? He had said goodbye to everyone and everything that mattered; the only thing that was not ready was his own scared heart. It was a bit like standing on the edge of one of the rocks out from Shuan, waiting to dive into deep water but not daring, not quite having the courage. Still, he had done all the important things.

He put off the light over his father's desk so that the only brightness now came from the fire. In those flames he could find all the faces – his grandfather's, Richard's, Rosie's. For a second they were there, like single photographs; then they were gone. The fire was falling grey again and there was no more wood.

'Remember what I was telling you earlier today.'

He jumped and turned quickly to see his father standing there. Duncan sat down in one of the armchairs and tickled Misty's throat as she immediately padded up for attention.

98

'It's not about success, you know, Cam – it's about finding your own way, what's right for you. I mean, if I had wanted a vast amount of money the last thing I'd have done was to try and dig it out of the soil at Ardnish!'

Cam thought about that and nodded in agreement.

'I know that, Dad,' he said, with a hint of indignation. 'It's not a danger I really worry about.'

'I know, but you should,' his father said; he leaned forward, his eyes bright. 'All I can say is that plenty of others have fallen for it before you, plenty of others who'd made up their minds they wouldn't go for money, no matter what it cost. And I'll tell you what made me think most about all of this, Cam. It was something that happened ages ago, when I was about your own age, down in the Borders. You know I've told you how I went to work on an estate down there when I was just out of agricultural college – it belonged to a man called Colonel Perry. Anyway, I really hated that place, couldn't wait to get back to the west coast! Colonel Perry himself was all right, but his wife – you should have seen the poor soul; she had no life in her face at all. She used to walk round the grounds as if she was sleepwalking, her eyes just full of sadness. Honestly, it used to haunt me; I could hardly bear in the end even to look at her. I'd go out of my way not to meet her; I'd feel this black weight come down on me. I don't know what was wrong with her; I suppose she suffered badly from depression. But d'you know what used to frighten me most of all? Looking around the place, I would think that she surely had everything in the world you could want! A beautiful mansion house, these amazing gardens, hills all around, their own stretch of river. A family too. You'd think someone with all that would have to be happy, but there she was in that sad state. It was as if she couldn't see one bit of it, was completely blind to the whole lot.

'It was terribly sad for her of course, but in a way it was really good for me – it made me think. Och, I had friends who were frantically chasing money; some were going to the cities, some in Scotland, some to London or abroad. There was one girl in fact I particularly didn't want to see going away...'

'Was that Peggy?' Cam smiled. He had heard stories about her all right.

'Aye,' his father said simply. 'Well, at one time I was tempted to go the same way. My dad was always on to me about work and

99

how I should get on, and not be stuck on the land like himself. It was as if it was some great shame to be a farmer! But after that, once I'd thought over everything having seen that poor lady for a whole year, I learned something; I learned to value what I had, what was important in life. I knew that more than even Peggy, I loved my home. Maybe I could have been a merchant banker in London, but every night I'd have been looking out of the window to catch a glimpse of the moon on Ben Luan! And if I couldn't have seen that, I couldn't have been happy. That's how it seemed to me, anyway.'

Duncan became silent; he wasn't a man given to such long speeches. Maybe he felt he'd said too much.

Cam just sat for a few moments staring into the fire, sorting out in his head what he wanted to say.

'It's a funny thing, Dad,' he said at last, 'but all these last days I've been thinking such a lot about stories. Different stories I've been told, by you and Grandpa and Mum and even Richard, all stories that have made up part of my life in different ways. It's as though all the important things are made up of stories, the things that matter to me. And I get this strange feeling that in a way they are all buried here, all around. D'you understand what I mean, or does it just sound daft?'

'Aye, I can understand, Cam. Maybe we need stories to explain life, to make it easier anyway. But I don't think they're only here. The reason you feel like that is because this is the only place you've ever lived! But there'll be stories in Aberdeen, stories beyond that, on and on; they won't go away, or cease to be, just 'cos you're leaving Ardnish! In a way they're like the folk you meet – some of them are good and some bad, and you have to choose which you want and leave the others behind. No one will take the ones at Ardnish away from you, that's for sure.'

Duncan struggled to his feet and yawned.

'I'd better get to my bed or I'll be good for nothing tomorrow! You come as well, Cam; your trouble is that you think too much – you were made that way, I suppose.'

Cam didn't answer, just smiled and said goodnight. The fire was down to nothing now, just a few blinks of orange in among the ash. He was hardly tired, but that was perhaps excitement more than anything else. He went over to the window and looked out.

The fields were deathly still; you could have lit a match and with so little breeze could have held it until it burned out. Quietly he opened the back door and went out on to the steps, not bothering with his jacket or even his boots although the stars were thick in the sky and it was freezing hard again. So cold, and still only October! At that moment he didn't feel split, but at last ready to leave. It was time to go, and he felt excited, even glad. He loved this place to death, but it would be here all right when he came back, and nothing and nobody could take it away from him.

Over the past few days he had done what he wanted to do, and he had made peace with himself. A harp had been found; he thought of it as a heart, a core that was beyond time, that would not decay. Once again he looked up and over the wood to Ben Luan, and seemed to see on it a strange light, a fire burning. But this time he was not frightened, for it was a long, long way away and was not calling him. He felt at that moment every yard between there and Ben Luan was a year, that his life stretched on unbelievably far.

And one day he, too, would be as a story, written into the land and remembered.